Praise for Jim Grimsley

"His is a unique voice . . . always compelling us, as readers, as audience, to enter his world for a time."   —*Southern Voice*

"There are few writers who sustain our attention through tone and voice. Jim Grimsley belongs in this elite group."
—Fred Chappell, *Raleigh News & Observer*

"His writing is both thoughtful and thought-provoking. His books are wrenching stories, magnificently told."   —*Just Out*

Praise for *Winter Birds*

"Remarkable . . . the story hits you in the gut."
—Michael Skube, *Atlanta Journal-Constitution*

"Tell everyone, I have rarely read anything as powerful. *Winter Birds* is altogether marvelous, so beautifully written I wanted to steal it and pretend it was mine, or go on tour reading it aloud so people could hear how getting it right makes your both hurt and happy, makes you cry out loud and sing praises simply that we are human."
—Dorothy Allison, author of *Bastard Out of Carolina*

"A story that blisters the sensibilities and shreds the heartstrings."
—Susan Lynne Harkins, *Orlando Sentinel*

"Extraordinarily vivid . . . written very close to the senses. The sights, sounds, smells, and feel of the country are wonderfully realized."
—Katharine A. Powers, *The Boston Globe*

"The violence is just half the story. The other half is the poetry that infuses *Winter Birds*. . . . A white-trash Southern landscape viewed from a gay perspective, with the bitterness of memory but also with unwavering, unsentimental love."   —*The New Yorker*

"Like a Greek tragedy, *Winter Birds* moves inexorably from its hypnotic opening to its final, chilling revelation, leaving the reader stunned, exhausted, and wonder-struck."

—Ron Carter, *Richmond Times-Dispatch*

"*Winter Birds* is a tough, loving book written with grace and restraint. It merits comparison to Steinbeck." —*Philadelphia City Paper*

"Read this book. It is a remarkable way to live for a while in the lives of people who must live these lives all the time."

—Ashby Brand Chowder, *Arkansas Democrat-Gazette*

"Grimsley has told an all-too-common tale of abuse with uncommon eloquence and endurance. His world is mesmerizing, blending icy horror with warm nostalgia. He shines a compassionate and understanding light on the unforgivable memories of the past. *Winter Birds* is his catharsis—and ours."

—Britt Reno, *The Virginian Pilot & Ledger Star*

"Grimsley has created a harrowing Southern gothic world, reminiscent of Faulkner or Caldwell. A remarkable first novel."

—George Needleman, *Booklist*

"One of the most beautifully written and emotionally passionate books I've read in years." —Rebecca Brown, *Seattle Weekly*

"I think I will not read another novel this year. Nothing else can be as vivid, as awful and awesome as this wonderfully harsh book. To turn the story of this harsh world into art, as Grimsley has, requires a sort of genius." —Max Steele, author of *The Hat of My Mother*

"This novel is as gripping as our hardest realities and as beautiful as our deepest loves." —Romulus Linney, author of *Holy Ghost*

"Jim Grimsley's *Winter Birds* is a disturbing and compassionate look at time, a family, and a place vividly real and meaningful."

—Horton Foote, author of *The Trip to Bountiful*

"Beautifully, eloquently written, with compassion addressing itself on every page." —*The Fort Worth Star-Telegram*

"Not since Dorothy Allison's award-winning *Bastard Out of Carolina* has there been such a moving picture of abuse and survival. This powerful little novel will take you places *Court TV* never could."

—Angie P. Howard, *Birmingham News*

"If there was a Richter scale with which to measure emotional intensity, *Winter Birds* would come in at 8.8 and the aftershocks would register for weeks afterward. If the line between love and hatred could be clearly discernible, *Winter Birds* would be its yardstick. If I were to write a novel, I would wish it to be half as fine as *Winter Birds*."

—Marilyn Chenault, *Vero Beach Press Journal*

Praise for *Dream Boy*

"Another potential award-winner. . . . Romantic passion, violence, and ultimate liberation coalesce in this singular display of literary craftsmanship."   —*Publishers Weekly*, starred review

"A powerful work that . . . leaves us with a powerful flavor and a flow of admiration."   —Fred Chappell, *Raleigh News & Observer*

"Grimsley proves once again that he can create believable characters and poignant situations that are resonant and heartfelt."

—*Winston-Salem Journal*

"*Dream Boy* is a powerful, fantastic novel."   —*The Columbia State*

"A tender . . . work of the soul that places Grimsley in the hallowed company of Baldwin, Carson McCullers in the school of emotional verisimilitude, and renders his story one to finish reluctantly and to part from never."   —Lawrence Schubert, *Detour* Magazine

"*Dream Boy* is unforgettable."   —*The Southern Pines Pilot*

"Superbly written . . . Grimsley writes with such quiet delicacy."

—*Detroit Free Press*

"Powerful."   —Elissa Schappell, *Vanity Fair*

Winter

Birds

Jim Grimsley

Scribner Paperback Fiction
Published by Simon & Schuster

SCRIBNER PAPERBACK FICTION
Simon & Schuster Inc.
Rockefeller Center
1230 Avenue of the Americas
New York, NY 10020

First Scribner Paperback Fiction edition 1997
Published by arrangement with Algonquin Books of Chapel Hill

SCRIBNER PAPERBACK FICTION and design are trademarks of Simon & Schuster Inc.

Designed by Bonnie Campbell
Manufactured in the United States of America

3 5 7 9 10 8 6 4

Library of Congress Cataloging-in-Publication Data
Grimsley, Jim, date.
Winter birds / by Jim Grimsley. —1st Scribner Pbk. Fiction ed.
p. cm.
Published first in the German translation, under the title "Wintervögel". St. Gallen/Berlin/São Paulo : Edition diá, 1992.
1. Family violence—United States—Fiction. 2. Hemophiliacs—United States—Fiction. 3. Boys—United States—Fiction.
4. North Carolina—Fiction. I. Title.
PS3557.R4949W56   1997
813'.54—dc20   96-8236
CIP

ISBN 0-684-82991-6

My thanks go to many people, but especially
to Del Hamilton, Faye Allen, my friends at
7Stages Theatre, Frank Heibert, Michael
Merschmeier, Thomas Brovot, Helmut and
the folks at *Edition diá*, Ann Marie Métailié,
Pierre Léglise-Costa, Lisa Corley, Kit Corley,
Greg Carraway, George Bacso, Susan Lindsay,
Roxanne Henderson, Nancy Mattox, Kathie
de Nobriga, Jo Carson, Celeste Miller, Elise
Witt, Madeleine St. Romain, Max Steele, Doris
Betts, Romulus Linney, Koukla MacLehose,
Jim Baker, Bill Whitehead, and my deepest
appreciation to Algonquin Books and
Workman. On a personal note, thanks to my
sister Jackie, my brother Jasper, and my late
brother Brian; also thanks to my stepfather
Don Hotaling and to Sarah, Kathryn, Corey,
and Janet. Deepest personal thanks to my
mother, for all the obvious reasons, and to
Carlos Schröder, for his great support and
friendship.

Contents

For Mary Brantham, my mother

The Airs

Out past the clapboard house in the weeds by the riverbank your brothers are killing birds. By the river flocks of
wrens, starlings and a few faded female cardinals have
gathered to feed on the leavings in the cornfield, and your
brothers lie hidden in the weeds with their shared gun,
waiting to burst open bird skulls with their copper BBs.
At every shot you can hear your brothers laughing.

You brush bits of powdered grass from your fingers.
You dread going to the river while your brothers are there,
so you wait till you see them walking home on the road
that divides the fields, three small figures swaggering
through the dirt. They handle the BB gun carelessly, trad-
ing it back and forth, each slinging the barrel over his
shoulder like a hunter in a frontier television show. You
walk toward them over furrows of earth littered with
cornstalks made soft by rain. By the edge of the dirt road
you meet them. They are shouting your name, asking if
dinner is ready yet. Grove, the youngest and littlest, grabs
the tail of your coat and turns you around. His swollen

arm is still in the pressure bandage. Watching him, you are glad you have no hurt places on you today. The gladness makes you ashamed. Grove's face, turned toward yours, is bright and happy in spite of his arm. "Will it snow today?" he asks. "I never saw snow before."

"Maybe so," you answer, watching the clouds overhead, hanging close over the treetops, heavy with a load of something waiting to fall. "The weatherman didn't say for sure. He only said it was likely."

Grove turns to Allen. "Tell Danny about the bird I killed. It was a little old wren wasn't it, Allen Ray?"

"Maybe it was a wren."

"I shot it right clean through the head, Danny!"

You do not smile but simply watch Allen, who shifts his feet. Before you can say anything, Allen flushes, as if he can already hear you scolding him. "You don't need to give me that high-and-mighty look. It didn't hurt Grove to shoot that gun. There ain't enough kick to it to bruise a spider."

"Does your arm hurt, Grove?"

"I don't care about this stupid arm, I hit that teeny bird right in the head."

"Probably it was a buzzard," Duck says, scowling toward the river, where the birds are chattering. "It was so far away you couldn't tell what it was. Probably it's not even dead."

"I saw it fall from way up in the air. I did too! You're jealous because you ain't killed one bird since we moved here, and you wasted a hundred-fifty BBs."

You tell them to hush. From the house you hear the sound you have come to escape. Duck, angry, says, "Don't tell me what to do, Mr. Big Shot."

"I said hush and be still."

He would go on arguing, you think, except he sees you are looking at the house across the field. They all fall quiet. Though their faces show no sign, you know how their bellies feel, the quick cool hollowness. The house is a square white box half hidden by trees. From it travels a flat thread of sound, and you feel yourself go empty listening to it. "It's Papa," you say. A raw edge to the wind's flight over the fields, a sound like an animal would make. Allen frowns and says, "We can all hear it. You don't have to tell us who it is."

Grove says, "Boy is he ever loud today."

"Don't talk about it," Allen says. "Act like it ain't there."

Duck clenches his fists against his ears. Grove says, "I bet Mama is scared already."

You say, watching Allen's hurt frown, "Be quiet Grove. We all know that."

"I bet she's walking the floors."

"Shut up," Duck says.

"I can't hear it any more," Allen says.

"It'll start again in a minute," you say.

"Quit acting like you're somebody's daddy—"

"Danny ain't acting like Papa!" Grove shouts.

"I ain't said he was acting like Papa," Allen says, "I said he was acting like somebody's daddy. It's a big difference." He steps on a cornstalk to make it crunch. Duck swings the BB gun across the stiff weeds. "Mama and Amy are alone with him," he says.

"I was just there," you answer. "He hasn't tried to hurt anybody."

"We should still go back there," Allen says.

"I don't want to go back there, I just came from there," you say. "I want to walk by the river."

"You go to that old river so much you ought to be a fish," Duck says.

"If you stay gone long you know Mama will get worried," Allen says. Grove laughs suddenly, clapping his hands. "Now who's acting like the daddy?"

"Danny knows she will."

You smell the hinted sweetness of the river water on the wind. You say, "I won't stay long. I promise."

Duck tosses the gun over his shoulder. "Danny can do what he wants to, who cares. But I ain't standing here all day in the freezing cold waiting for him to make up his mind."

"Well you better be careful with that gun," Allen says. "Because I ain't going to fix it any more if you break it." He takes Grove's hand and they begin to walk toward the house. "You don't fall on nothing else to get it started bleeding either. That would be all Mama could stand."

"Yes Papa Allen, yes Papa Allen," Grove chants, and dances over the corn rows behind the others. They kick a path through the stalks, shouting at each other. You stand there listening until the low clouds and the distance shrink them and drink their noises. Beyond them, washed in filtered light, the house they walk toward huddles against the edges of the fields. You already feel it waiting for you to come back.

But you turn away, Danny the Lesser, and you ease toward the walls of pine whispering, "I will never go home, I will never go home." You walk to the river to listen to the slow water drift between the banks, hoping you will find a place there to hide from this noise that begins again now, traveling low to the ground.

Danny the Lesser

Today is Thanksgiving and you are freed from school. You can lie in your bed of honeysuckle vine and dream all day beside the river. Walking there, you hug yourself with thin arms, your dark hair blown by the wind. Overhead the branches sway back and forth. At night when you lie awake in your bed you can hear the wind sing in their tops, and the sound makes you believe a person lives in each tree.

As you walk you dread the things you have learned to dread: your Papa, your special blood, anything that shakes it. You place each step carefully so you do not fall.

Round a curve in the path Queenie sniffs this way and that in the grass, swinging her bony head. Maybe she is smelling to see where your brothers have gone. She sees you and runs to you with her tongue trailing in the grass. River smell clings to her fur. You hug her close, hearing her heartbeat, stroking her soft brown coat. When she lifts her wet nose to be scratched you scratch it.

Her distended belly sways back and forth, heavy with

the puppies she waits to have. You scratch the taut skin of her belly lightly, half-expecting it to make the sound balloons make when you rub their sides. Delighted, she rolls on her back, tail thumping dirt. Her naked white belly is hairless and smooth, and you touch it gingerly. Puppies sleep under this warm skin. Queenie watches you as if she expects this is the beginning of some new game. You say, "Don't worry, I won't try to get them out before they're done. I only wondered what colors they are."

She settles her head in the dry grass. You touch her pink nipples, the stiff tips hot and moist. "Mama says she's going to drown your babies in the river," you tell her. "Grove says he won't let her get your babies, he says he'll hide them as soon as they're born, but Mama will find them wherever they are. She says she don't want stray dogs around her house eating up everything in sight. Not when she's already feeding their stray mama."

Queenie cocks her ear. Babies are easy to get, she says. I'm not scared of your Mama. I can make as many babies as I want to.

"You don't even care about your babies, do you?"

They're just babies, she says.

"But where do you get your babies from? And why do they feel so hot when I touch your belly?"

They're about to burn right slam up inside me, she says, with her tongue trailing into the grass.

At school the girls say puppies come from the same place babies come from, they slide into their mama's stomachs out of the sky, easy as snowflakes melting in your hand. Never mind what the nasty boys say. "But how do they get out of your stomach?"

She gives you an arrogant glance. Why they climb out, stupid. That's how.

She touches your hand with a paw cold from being on the ground. She wishes you would rub her belly some more, but suddenly you are tired of this hungry look she gives you and you wonder if anybody could ever pet her enough to satisfy her. Mama would tell you to stop touching the dog this way. You say, "Go away stupid dog, I don't want to rub on you any more."

But she goes on waiting for your hand. You stand and push her with your shoe. "Get up from that ground you stupid thing. Go away from me, you don't belong to my family and you never did and you never will either!"

When she still does not move you walk away from her. She simply watches you with her round black eyes, her pale belly pointing to the sky.

YOU THINK the pines must like the quiet, the same way God likes quiet in church, so you tiptoe through the underbrush. Under your breath you sing, "Shall we gather at the ri-i-ver—" breaking off the tip of a branch as you always do when you pass a low tree or bush—"the beautiful, beautiful ri-i-ver," you sing, stripping the leaves off the stems, tearing them to pieces and dropping the pieces to the ground. You love the way the bits of leaves fall, the air under them so solid it knocks them from side to side.

But soon you stop your wandering and walk directly

to the river, not caring how much noise your feet make in the beds of cold-stiffened leaves. You have a place you always go, a certain clearing beside a train trestle that you found the first day your family moved to this house. You like the place because the branches overhead are thin and sunlight, on a clear day, falls through them making nets of shadow on the ground. Today same as every other day something in you lifts as you enter the clearing. You jump over a fallen log imagining Mama warning you to be careful, don't fall on something and get yourself hurt. You sing the song louder, "Shall we ga-ather at the ri-i-ver, the be-oo-tiful, be-oo-tiful ri-i-ver!"

To the nearest tree you say, "Tree, now you better warn me if my Papa comes, so I have plenty of time to hide."

The wind off the cold river cuts through you and you squeeze your thin coat tight. You gaze at the surface of the river, leaves spinning downstream like music box dolls. Honeysuckle grows thick as a mattress on the riverbank, and you lie on it looking up at the sky.

This is what you came here for, to lie here like this, to watch the clouds for a while and then to count: one two three, shut things away: shut away the house and the flat fields, shut away Mama Papa Amy Kay Allen Duck Grove shut them away! You are an orphan, you live in these woods away from them all, away from the whole world, your family is dead shut them away . . .

You close your eyes. You have come to the river to dream, a dream whose shadows move against your lids.

YOU DREAM the River Man again: River Man comes out of the water to your honeysuckle mattress on the bank. He is broad as an oak tree and strong as a bear, tall and brown-skinned with shaggy black hair. He lives in the water or in the forest where you have wandered. He calls you his son. You know no one else in the world, only him. You have no other home, only his home. You see in his eyes every minute how he cares for you.

You live in a dark room, maybe a cave. When you picture the room, the walls are dark like packed earth, lit by torches. The light they give and the shadows they cast make the room seem warm and safe. The furs of large animals hang on the walls. In one corner of the room a fire burns, smoke drifting up a stone chimney. You have seen rooms like this on television, in movies about the jungle man and the boy he raises as his own child. When he is in the room with you, you can always hear the slow steady rhythm of his breathing.

The room has a secret entrance that only you and River Man know about, an underwater tunnel that you both swim through.

Lying here today you can remember a dozen adventures you have had with River Man—paddling a canoe down river with him, past crocodiles sliding off the slick banks, past submerged rocks that raise their heads and turn out to be hippopotamuses—walking with River Man through the ruins of a forgotten city, building after empty building—you alone another time, lost somewhere in the forest or along the river, anxious because River Man doesn't

know where you are. You try to find him, walking endlessly along the shore calling River Man, River Man . . .

Sometimes you dream of running through the forest,
which you imagine to be infinite, you delighting in the
motion of your running and in the fact that each step you
take is as silent as the last, a mere whisper over the blades
of grass.

Sometimes you see animals and stroke their soft
hides: gazelle, antelope, small monkeys, baby lions, all
calm at the touch of your hands, as if you are magical.

Sometimes you climb into the wide-branched trees,
leaping light-footed from one tree to the next, a monkey or
a squirrel yourself, running alone in the light and the solid
masses of leaves.

Today you dream you sit beside River Man on the
riverbank. You have raced him here. He laughed when
you beat him like he always does. He says, You're getting
faster and faster, his voice warm and deep.

—You could have beat me if you wanted to. I know
you could.

—How does your leg feel? He glances at your thigh.
You shake your head and answer, It doesn't hurt. None of
the cuts came open.

—I shouldn't have let you go so fast, I was afraid—
He breaks off a leaf from a low reed and looks away, troubled. You say you feel fine, the leg is healing, and you look
down at it yourself. But even though this is your dream
that you are making even you aren't prepared for what you
see.

You dream the leg is pitted and scabbed. You picture it perfectly. Along one side of the thigh ribbons and threads of clotted blood mesh with pale cut flesh. The cuts have closed now, but you can remember them raw and open, the red running away, free.

The deep tearing.

YOU REMEMBER how it happened from another dream another day, that you go over again from start to finish now.

Alone in the brilliant noon forest, you part the leaves with your hand.

A clearing ahead, bright gold as a bowl of sunlight, ringed with dense brush, the grass emerald-colored, thick broad blades.

The sky above the clearing broad as a valley of blue, engulfing everything.

You must go into that light from this darkness, this protection.

The cool river lost somewhere miles behind, through thicknesses of leaves and underbrush; River Man there somewhere, far away.

You must no longer travel hidden, you must enter this clearing to learn how this light feels on the skin.

But the thought of standing naked beneath that nakedness has made your throat go dry.

You step into the light, parting the leaves and branches with your hand. Your shadow shrinks beneath you. The sunlight is a new thing to your skin, a tingling that is fresh and filling—you smile, you run forward through the high grass, your too-quick heartbeat all that shows of your fear.

The clearing is a circle and you stand in the middle, turning around and around.

The sky is a wheel, you are under the hub, the hub is an eye looking down as you look up.

When you hear the new sound behind you, at first you don't turn to it.

Then you hear the sound again and know what it is: the muffled rumble from the wide throat.

When you turn you see it.

Bright lion, loping large-thighed across the grass, almost playful.

You bury your hands in his mane.

The wide mouth yawns.

The vast paw lifts, a playful tap.

You gasp at the tearing, lean away still gripping the mane, you shudder and step away slowly, heart exploding in bursts of heat—the lion eager, pressing toward you, warm red tongue on your hands.

You lead him to the side, steps coming hard for you as he leaps high, suspended in the air above the high grass that brushes your thigh; stained after with the luminous blood streaming down.

You limp but never fall.

Bright lion calms beside you, no longer leaping.

You reach the trees and he watches you climb one of them, the pain like a fire in your side. He sits on his haunches and lashes his tail, puzzled that you don't want to play any more. You fall into the crooked hollow of a branch too high even for his highest leap.

The smell of your blood drifts out into the air.

Bright lion watches from below.

YOU DREAM you waken in River Man's cave to the sound of water lapping in the tunnel. Shadows move on the earth walls. From a torch? No, from the fire burning in the stone fireplace.

Your leg hurts the same as it would hurt if you were having a bleed there. When you touch it dried blood breaks off in flakes, leaving a light stain on your fingers. You remember the lion now, and falling asleep in the crook of a tree like a monkey.

—River Man?

Your voice so small the room swallows it.

—River Man, are you here anywhere?

As you waken fully you realize you lie in River Man's bed, not your own. The room looks funny from this angle, everything out of place and yet not out of place. When you try to move your leg it burns, and pain like fire shoots up your side. But you ignore it, leaning over the side of the bed till you can see your own bed, hidden behind a wooden chest in the corner.

He lies there, a big shadow, feet hanging off the edge. You hear his breathing now, barely, so deep it almost makes no sound. You say, River Man, but softer, not meaning to wake him, only wanting to use his name. But he rises and looks at you.

—Danny? Danny, you're awake?

—How come it's so cold in here?

He crosses the room and says hi, hand on your forehead. He looks tired. He says, You are cold.

—Cover me up with something. He gets a blanket, something heavy, maybe the fur of a big animal, a bear or a lion he killed. He spreads it over you and you sigh at its engulfing heaviness and warmth.

He says, The bleeding finally stopped a little while ago.

—My leg feels big.

—It's swollen some. The cuts are the worst. No tearing, only deep slashes.

—It was a lion, River Man.

—I know.

—He was gold-colored, and his mane was so bright it looked like it was on fire. He came running out of the woods like he wanted to play.

He turns his face toward the fire.—I know that too.

—You saw him?

—I saw him later, yes. He watches you for a long time, and at last touches your shoulder tenderly.—I didn't think the bleeding would ever stop. Do you know how scared I was?

You have no answer to that. He watches you and smiles. Touching your forehead, he says, You're still cold.

—I'll be all right now.

—You need better than that, he says, and rises up tall and dark, a warm shadow, lifting the fur and sliding beside you.

NOW THE dream goes away. When you open your eyes the river flows past you just as before, and the branches overhead still weave the mazes that slow the falling light. The trestle hangs over the river waiting for a train. You wipe the seat of your pants when you stand, and throw a stick deep into the river, thinking it would be fun to spin like that stick spins, or like those leaves, twirling on top of the water till the river runs into the sea.

The dream has left you with a feeling of heaviness.

You walk down the riverbank, balancing at the edge of the weed fringe, looking down into the water at your own face staring up. "You're ugly," you tell your reflection, and you drop a stone into yourself. "You got a face like a hoe cake and crooked teeth and big ears."

You chant names whose sounds you like: Genesis Exodus Leviticus Numbers Deuteronomy Eleanor River Potter's Lake Mars Hill Matthew Mark Luke MenthoEucalyptus Song of Solomon Isaiah Jeremiah Hezekiah Daniel Nicholas Crell Bobjay Crell Robert Jay Crell Robert Jay Judas Robert Judas. Crell. Then you declare to your own bare arms, "You're so white you might as well be a ghost."

Always you watch where you step, checking to make sure there's no glass underfoot, nothing to turn your ankle on, no place to fall. You keep your back to the places where the underbrush is thin, where you might glimpse the house across the fields. Your family is dead, dead, you are an orphan . . .

But the pines cannot hold back Papa's voice. When you hear it you stand still. The wind increases, drowning the noise for a moment and bending the pines back and forth, now slow, now faster. The clouds hang low against the pine tops. Far across the field you see Queenie with her nose in the dirt. Beyond her the house shines. You think maybe your Mama stands at one of the windows, looking out the way she likes to. Maybe she has been waiting for you. Maybe she sees you now and is glad you're coming home. Maybe that is even her shadow you see now, turning away from one of the black squares of glass.

Or maybe it is Papa who watches.

For a moment you want to go back to the river. But no. You will take River Man with you, you will dream he walks beside you across the fields, brown and tall and strong, his warm hand on your shoulder.

The Catalog

of Houses

In those days, Danny, you slept in the same room with your brothers and Amy Kay, in the same bed with Allen, who would never let you lie close to him unless he was cold. The house by the river was always cold, wind pouring in through cracks under the doors, around the windows, down chimneys and out boarded-up fireplaces. The family that farmed these fields once lived in this house, but they sold the land long ago and the new owner doesn't even remember their name.

You moved to this house a little over a month ago, the seventh house you have lived in since you were born. After you move out of this house you will live in seven others with your family, before you are old enough to make your home wherever you choose.

You and Amy Kay named this house right away — you called it the Circle House because the doors opened in a circle and you could walk from room to room forever. Amy Kay and you named all the houses you lived in, though finding the right name wasn't always easy.

The two of you began the game in the Snake House, a green cinder-block cottage with a red shingle roof. Mama liked that house better than any of the places you moved to later because in that house the living room and hall were paneled in polished cherry wood, and because the kitchen had cabinets built into the walls.

The Snake House stood in a thicket of loblolly pine at the edge of a patch of woods where snakes abounded. The house was built on a low foundation, and snakes could crawl into it through holes in the cinder block that Mama plugged as best she could with bits of stone and old rags. Later, when you are older, Mama will tell you stories about the snakes she found in the house. Once, she opened the hall closet to get down a set of sheets and in fact had her hand on the edge of one folded sheet when she saw a black snake coiled on top, darting fire at her with its tongue. The snake vanished as soon as she stepped back from the closet.

After counting her breaths to ten, she searched the closet from top to bottom, lifting every sheet and towel slowly and carefully off the shelves. She found no snake even when the closet was empty, so she searched the rest of the house, spilling clothes out of chests of drawers, pulling couches and chairs away from the walls, even rolling up the worn piece of carpet in her bedroom, thinking the snake might have hidden beneath it. Still she found no snake anywhere.

She went to the bathroom—when she got nervous about something she had to pee every five minutes, she said. She had sat down on the toilet with her pants around her ankles when she saw the snake beside her in the bathtub, tasting the edge of the drain with its tongue. Mama ran out of the bathroom pulling up her pants and snatched the garden hoe from its place next to the back door. She chopped off the snake's black head while it frantically tried to fit itself down the drain.

Another time she heard a dry crawling sound under the sink and spent the rest of the morning taking everything out of drawers and off shelves until at noon she found a chicken snake curled behind the drainpipes. She crushed its head with a tub of lard and burned its body on the trash pile along with the rest of the day's refuse.

Another time Mr. Luther, who owned the seed farm Papa worked on and the house you lived in, shot a six-foot rattlesnake in the dirt road near your mailbox. Mama, Amy Kay, and you watched from behind the ditch. Mama held you by the shoulder to keep you from running into the road. You watched the dying snake whip dust with its thick, musical tail. The sight of the long thing lashing frightened you so much Mama had to sit with you that night before you could fall asleep.

Later that same summer, as Mama folded clothes she had gathered sun-drenched from the line, Amy Kay called out to her, "Mama, there's a snake with Danny on the bed!" Mama ran to the door.

You simply sat there, Danny, staring at what might have been a coil of dull brown rope. Mama whispered to you not to move. Later when she told the story she said she was terrified at the way you sat so perfectly motion-less, staring with complete fascination at the snake. She brought a quilt from the other room. She stepped calmly behind the snake and threw the quilt over the dry, scaled body. Without pausing to take a breath she pulled you off the bed—you stiff and wide-eyed, not making a sound — and then she balled up the bedspread around the quilt and the furious snake and dragged the whole bundle out-side. The snake coiled round and round itself in the fabric. She let it find its own way out and cut off its head with the hoe, cut its body a dozen other places, watching the pieces of snake turn over and over helplessly in the grass. A moccasin. Inside, she stripped you raw and checked every inch of you for bites. You held her arm and gazed at her without a word. Amy Kay watched from the doorway, knuckles in her mouth.

That night Mama told Papa in a high, strained voice, "You better get Mr. Luther to stop up the holes in this house. I don't care if it takes iron bars to do it, if that's what it takes to keep the snakes away from my babies." When Papa held her she trembled. He asked, more gently than was his habit, what had happened this time.

Whether he ever spoke to Mr. Luther about the snakes is another matter. Papa had work to do and no time to worry about snakes. He was the foreman on Mr. Luther's farm and the work kept him busy from morning till night. It was here on Mr. Luther's seed farm that Papa lost most of one arm.

You never heard the whole story, Danny, and neither

did your brothers or your sister. Papa never talked about that day, and only rarely mentioned the green cinder-block house or Mr. Luther's farm. Mama told you the story. She said she was hanging out clothes on the line when she saw Mr. Luther's blue Cadillac full of people roaring away from the fields in a fog of gray dust. She figured something was wrong by the speed of the car and thought maybe Mr. Luther was having another heart attack. It made her sad to think so because Mr. Luther had always been nice to her. But she went on hanging out the clothes, expecting she would hear whatever news there was when Papa came home for lunch.

A few minutes later Mrs. Luther drove up in the white Cadillac. Mrs. Luther got out of the car slowly, as if she weren't quite sure where she was. Her face was ashen. There was an accident, she said, or something like that, not meeting Mama's eyes. God only knew how it happened, Bobjay knew to turn off the harvester before he tried to clean it. Mama dropped her load of clothes to the ground and grabbed Mrs. Luther by the arm. Mrs. Luther reared back like a snake about to strike. "Mr. Luther has taken him to the hospital himself," she said. "There wasn't time for an ambulance. Bobjay was working alone in the backfields and got his arm caught in the corn harvester— it ground up half his arm."

Mama released the woman and turned slowly. Mrs. Luther watched her without any particular sympathy. "They brought him to my house. Right into my kitchen when any fool could have seen there wasn't a thing I could do for him. There's blood everywhere. The boys said he walked half a mile through the fields with only his shirt for a tourniquet. Mr. Luther said I should drive you to the hospital as soon as the boys get back from the fields."

"The boys?" Mama asked. Mrs. Luther took a long deep breath. "My husband sent three of them back there to get the . . . to clean the . . . out of the machine."

A MONTH or so later you moved to a red-shingled house that smelled of fish. Mama found this house for you to move into after Mr. Luther told her Papa couldn't work on the farm anymore with only the one arm that he could use. Mama sold her wedding rings to pay the first month's rent. Mr. Luther's hands loaded your furniture on a truck while Papa sat in the car smoking cigarettes and staring ahead at the empty driveway. Mama watched him nervously and hollered at the men loading the truck to be careful with her furniture.

The new house was hardly a house at all, having only one large room with a window in each wall and a sink in the corner. The outhouse stood in lush weeds a short walk out the back door, down a path fringed with chickweed and sheep's burr. You children had never used an outdoor toilet before and at first you were afraid you would fall through one of the dark, stinking holes. But Mama told you this was the only kind of bathroom there was when she was little, and she stayed with you the first time, holding you steady with one hand while covering her eyes with the other.

You named this place the Fish House, because before you lived in it the owner Mrs. Edna Crenshaw had run a fish store in the building, and the smell of the fish had soaked every board. Mrs. Crenshaw, a large, powder-fleshed woman, had been in the fish market business many years, buying fresh seafood off trucks that drove straight up the highway from the coast. Her customers were the local farmers and merchants, who got tired of their wives' fried chicken and fatback and greasy pork chops. Over the years Mrs. Crenshaw had done well enough to lay aside money to build herself a brand-new brick fish store across the highway from the old one. You could see it from the window of your house, a small, square brick building with a multicolored sign in front, that Mrs. Crenshaw's husband retouched lovingly every week from the same four cans of paint. Amy Kay called him Mr. Fish Face because of the way his eyelids drew back from his eyeballs, exposing the whites all around.

You and Amy shared a bed in one corner of the house, with Allen's crib next to you near the couches and chair that separated you from Mama and Papa's bed in the other corner of the house. The first night you lived there Mama unpacked dishes while Papa glared at her from that bed. His empty sleeve dangled at his side. "This whole place smells like goddamn fish," he said.

Mama settled the dishes in the fresh-scrubbed cabinets without answering or looking around. From the frown on Papa's face you knew there would be a fight that night. It gave you a feeling in your stomach, a hurting like you wanted to cry inside. You watched Papa and waited. When he began to shout—about the bitch who couldn't find no better place to live than this shack a fat-ass Holiness woman sold fish out of —you ran for the screen door to escape the sound. You tripped and fell. No one noticed then. You sat outside in the cold, listening to Papa's shouts till long after dark. Mama unpacked boxes and wiped her eyes. Finally Papa drank enough to fall asleep in his chair. You came back into the house then. But even after Mama put Papa to bed and turned out the last light in the house you lay awake in your bed, listening.

In the morning your ankle was swollen where you had fallen. Mama put a cold cloth full of ice against the hurt place, and stroked your forehead. "The doctors say your blood is special," she said. "It doesn't do what other people's blood does. Isn't it nice to have special blood? Even when it hurts a little?"

Papa, frowning and sullen behind her, looked at your ankle as if it were untouchable. When the wound in his piece of arm healed Papa took a job at a gas company paying thirty-five dollars a week. He delivered bottles of gas for farm wives to cook with, and bulk loads of gas for farm husbands to cure tobacco with, and repaired stoves and furnaces and refrigerators besides. Even with one hand Papa could fix almost anything, if he had time to fiddle with it. He got a little happier when he was working again. But he wasn't making nearly as much money as he had made working for Mr. Luther. Every night you ate potatoes cooked a different way. Papa hardly ever spoke at all, only stared at his plate. In his presence you children became quiet and fearful, because he was always frowning, and because the place where his whole arm used to be looked vacant and strange now. He would catch you looking at him and turn away. Where before he came home drunk once in two weeks, now he came home drinking two or three times a week. The look in his eyes was like flat gray stone.

Mama watched him carefully from across that one big room, continually gauging the distance.

No neighbors came to visit, except Mrs. Crenshaw at the first of each month, standing in the door wearing her smile and her blood-stained apron, talking jovially about Holiness revivals, holding out her dough-white hand for Mama to count green money onto. Mama watched the money slide into Mrs. Crenshaw's apron pocket and Mrs. Crenshaw turned away, wiping her hands on that apron. Until one month Mama met her with a smile, no money. Papa had to pay on the hospital bill for his arm, Mama said, or else the hospital would arrest him. So could Mrs. Crenshaw wait a little while for the rent? A week or two?

Mrs. Crenshaw, being a woman of firm business principle, shook her head no. Only a little later you moved again, away from the Fish House.

AMY NAMED the next house the Ice House because there was only one heater in the whole place, in the kitchen. All winter you and the others sat there watching television till it was time to go to bed, with the rest of the rooms closed off and dark around you, too cold to live in. Allen Raymond had grown big enough now to sit up on Mama's lap and suck his thumb; you couldn't call him a baby any more. But Mama was going to have another baby soon. Her stomach was growing bigger and bigger.

Mama and Papa argued the whole winter about this baby that was coming. Papa didn't see how Mama could expect to feed another mouth on forty dollars a week, which was what he was making now that he had worked for the gas company for a while. Mama asked what Papa expected her to do about it now. It was water under the bridge. The new baby was on the way, they couldn't do anything but love it. Papa said, expensive love, if we all have to go hungry to feed it.

Later you watched him standing in the doorway to their bedroom, staring at the stump of his arm and grinding his jaw. You understood their fights only vaguely, but you knew that the strange dulled look on Papa's face meant he had been drinking from the bottle Mama hated. He drank from that bottle more and more as Mama's stomach grew. Through the cold months their arguments blended one into the other.

Once he came home late in the night with a cut over one eye and a story about a fight in the Downs, the part of Potter's Lake where black people lived. Papa said some coon cut him with the lid of a tomato can. The sheriff's deputy broke up the fight before it went any farther, but since he was a friend of Papa's he didn't arrest anybody. Mama tended the cut and put Papa to bed, glad he had picked somebody else to fight for an evening. He slept like a lamb till the next afternoon, curled up like a baby under mounds of quilts. A frost-covered Sunday slipped by, Papa laughing and joking with all of you.

The next week Amis John Crell was born. Papa drove Mama to the hospital in his work truck. Mama's youngest sister Delia stayed in the house with you children, sleeping in Amy Kay's rickety bed, in the same room with Allen and you. Mama stayed in the hospital four nights running. Papa visited her at first, but he didn't like hospitals and never stayed for very long. At night when he came home he talked to Delia in a low voice and gave her long looks you didn't understand. But they made you feel afraid. Delia was always careful to keep you children in the room with her and to ask about Mama and the baby. She went to bed when you children went to bed, and locked the bedroom door, but once she stood beside it listening for a long time.

The hospital bill totaled five hundred forty-nine dollars and seventy-three cents.

When it came in the mail Papa read it and left the house without a word. You watched him splash on the headlights and roar out of the yard, his face hard and angry, his whitened knuckles gripping the steering wheel. Amy, Allen, and you fell asleep before he came home. But every hour Mama tiptoed into the room to check on the new baby that slept like a little pink nut inside his shell of blankets. Whenever Mama came in the room you woke up and watched her standing over the crib with that tender look on her face.

Early in the morning Papa came home and the argument began. The shouting woke you up too, and you listened. Pretty soon Amis John began to cry because of the noise, but when Mama tried to comfort him Papa chased her out of the room and wouldn't let her come back inside. You heard her call out once in pain. All night the baby sobbed, with only Amy, Allen, and you to quiet him. In the morning Mama's face was swollen on one side and her eye was dark blue. Papa sat at the kitchen table drinking his coffee as if nothing had happened. When he left Mama took Amis John to her room and they stayed there all day with the door closed.

In the spring after the second winter in the house, Papa found a place he thought was better, and you moved again.

IN THE Pack House Amis John got his nickname—Duck— by taking his first steps through a mudhole. He had his share of cuts and bruises but they healed quickly, and the doctors soon declared him as normal as Allen before him as far as bleeding was concerned. Mama breathed easier when she found that out. Even with a new baby she watched you every minute, Danny, and you never stepped out of the house without hearing her warning to be careful. You were always careful. You never walked barefoot in the grass. For a while your spells of bleeding didn't come so often. You were happy, listening to Mama sing as she changed Duck's diapers, calling Amy Kay or you to come hold the pins.

After moving to a new house Papa was always calm for a while, as if in finding a new place to live he accomplished something that eased his mind. But this house was particularly ugly. Mama said it looked like it hadn't been painted in forty years. Amy and you took turns finding bits of old paint on the clapboards outside. You couldn't tell what color the house had been, though Amy swore it was powder blue. Amy studied the Sears catalog and knew what all the colors were. The house had three rooms standing side by side: a kitchen and two bedrooms, with a porch in the back. Behind a grove of saplings stood the outhouse, surrounded by mint-green grass and lush goldenrod.

That spring Papa paid three hundred dollars for an old brown Ford with half a seat in the back. Mama put a three-legged stool there in place of the missing half-seat and told Amy Kay always to sit there because it was her special place. Because of his arm Papa had to drive with a steering knob. But he never let Mama drive when he was with her.

To help pay for the car Mama got farm work, and because there was no place for you to go, you all went to work with her. In the early months of spring she helped a farmer down the road set out his baby tobacco plants into the fields. In the summer she worked with the other women in the neighborhood tying the green tobacco on sticks so it could be hung in barns to be cured. You children played in the fields near the women and their trucks of green tobacco. You remember the hats the women wore, bright-colored straw sun hats with wide brims and striped strings that tied under the women's soft chins. The women rolled their pants past their pale, dimpled knees. Mama's hat was blue as a robin's egg and her string was striped red and white. On one of her knees was a small purple scar from a fight with one of her brothers during which he hit her with a garden hoe. Her white legs freckled in the sun, never turning an even shade of brown like the other women. Mama laughed and talked with the women all day long, waiting for the tractor or the mules to drag another creaking truck of tobacco from the fields. She had a different way of looping the tobacco onto the stick than the local women were used to, Mama having grown up in Pike County near Madisonville, hours away from Potter's Lake. The Potter's Lake women always watched her work, remarking that they sure couldn't judge why people around here thought there was only one way to do a job when lo and behold here was Ellen Crell proving that people in different parts of the world could do the same job a different way. It was a revelation.

You children wandered in and out of the barns, smelling the dry, bitter leaves and wondering what the big companies did to the tobacco to make cigarettes out of it. Amy Kay said they took all the dry leaves and made a big heap and then hired teams of horses to walk on the heap till there was nothing left but crushed powder. Which worked all right, Amy said, except sometimes the horses pissed on the tobacco, which was why some cigarettes had filters on them. Most days Amy stayed in the shade of the barn tending Duck, who grinned at her from his blanket and made soft noises in his throat. Amy talked to him all day long, giving him her finger to play with and generally treating him as if he were a friend with whom she was conducting a serious, private conversation.

For dinner you rode home in the truck and ate chicken Mama fried that morning, or else scrambled eggs and fatback, or macaroni and tomatoes, or whatever could be quickly cooked. By the time you sat at the table your faces ran with sweat from the kitchen heat. Mama kept a fly swatter next to her chair and used it during the meal, flicking the dead flies into the trash bag next to the stove. In a good week she could earn as much money as Papa. Together they stretched the dollars to cover the groceries and the rent and the car, and sometimes even farther than that to pay for the car insurance or pieces of the hospital bills.

That fall Amy Kay started school. Mama drove you all to Gibsonville to buy Amy's school clothes. You and Allen watched the two of them discuss dresses and shoes and prices, Mama bending to listen to Amy as seriously as if Amy were as tall and old as she. The tobacco money slid through Mama's fingers into various cash register drawers. Since Mama carried Duck, Amy carried the bags, now and then stopping to admire her new things.

Mama and Papa took her to school together the first day. Later when she came home Amy said school was fun, except the girl's bathroom was so big she like to got lost in it. Once it was clear to you that Amy could always come home when school was over, it didn't seem like such a big deal any more.

Soon after, in the autumn, Mama took in cured tobacco to grade, to make extra money. She cleared off the back porch and used the free space to house the sticks of dry, acrid-smelling leaves, sorting them into bundles according to the color and quality of the leaf. You helped her by taking the tobacco off the sticks. She tied the bundles of graded leaves at the top with a single soft leaf, tight as the handkerchiefs black women tied around their hair. The smell of the dry tobacco filled the house. When she was finished with one load it was packed in the back of the farmer's truck and another load deposited on the porch.

Papa watched Mama work when he came home at night. He would gaze at her fingers, quick and deft in the dusty piles of leaves, an angry, sullen look on his face. He would try to make her stop working and pay attention to him. "Why don't you come in the house and talk to me," he would say, "I haven't had anybody to talk to all day," and she would stop sometimes, if he was in a good mood, if she didn't think the talk would end up in another fight.

Winter came. This house proved as cold as the one before it, so Papa started to look for another place and soon found a house he thought was a better bargain. Mama didn't always agree with Papa's opinion of a house, but that time she told him the place was much nicer. She needed to keep him in the best mood she could manage.

Somehow that winter she would have to tell him she thought she was pregnant again. .

In early December you moved to the Blood House.

THE BLOOD House stood in a confusion of tobacco barns, tool sheds, and rusted farm equipment, and had been used as a pack house for dried tobacco the last fifteen years, according to the farmer who owned it. This gentleman, Mr. Silas Henry Rejenkins, sported a belly that ballooned over his empty belt loops. None of his shirts, whether they buttoned down or pulled over, reached far enough to cover all of this vast fleshy melon. His navel, exposed to every kind of weather, sunk like a gulch into his soft, hairy stomach. The first day Amy and you saw him waddling about the farmyard Amy told you, "I bet that old man puts boogers in his bellybutton."

Mr. Rejenkins agreed to rent Papa the house for next to nothing, provided Papa would let Mr. Rejenkins store cured tobacco in the rooms you didn't use, for Mama to grade and bundle. Papa agreed to the arrangement but he didn't much like it. Mr. Rejenkins paid too much attention to Mama from the start. The day after you moved into the house Mr. Rejenkins knocked on the door first thing in the morning, to see whether Mama was satisfied with the condition of the house, he said. Though the morning was cold he smelled of sweat. Every few minutes he hitched up his pants to keep them from sliding off his slab of belly. When he smiled you counted his jagged yellow teeth. Amy Kay said from the way his clothes looked he must dress before he went to bed and sleep in them to get that many wrinkles. But someone took wonderful care of his shoes. They shone so bright you might have seen your reflection in the patent leather tips. The waxed black laces tied in a lopsided bow.

That first morning he kept looking down at his shoes and then looking at Mama, as if he expected her to say something about them. Mama was polite as she led him through the chilled rooms, showing him the ripped-out back door screen and the broken lock on the back door. She pointed out in her most formal voice that without a lock and a good screen on the door she could hardly feel safe in the house. She showed him the leaky ceilings in two of the bedrooms, which would rot the roof if he weren't careful. She indicated the loose floorboards in the kitchen, which had already caused her to stumble when she was unpacking her pots and pans. Suppose she had been carrying hot soup instead? Mama pointed out the broken windows in the living room, kitchen, and bed-rooms, which were dangerous for her children, she said, and especially for you. She explained to him about the trouble with your blood, sounding out the name for it, *hemophilia*, and holding you in front of her hopefully. Mr. Rejenkins smiled at everything and watched you only vacantly. You might have been some kind of farm dog. Mama said she hoped Mr. Rejenkins would see to these repairs she had mentioned as soon as he could. Mr. Rejenkins smiled and gazed down at his shoes again.

In the light from the kitchen window the shoes

sparkled and shone. Mama thought they must be new and he must want someone to praise them, so she paid him a politeness on the subject of new shoes in general. He favored her with a slow wink, as if this were the first word anyone had said since he walked through the door. "These are my Sunday shoes, honey, I've had them near two years. My wife she takes real good care of them." He smiled slowly. "I wished she would take that good a care of everything."

Soon after, Papa told Mama over breakfast he thought the fat buzzard took an awful lot of trouble to fix up a shack for fifteen dollars a month rent. Mama said it wasn't any knowing what people would do. Papa said the house had been sitting empty fifteen years and here all of a sudden he would rent it dirt cheap and then fix it up all nice and pretty by himself. It didn't make any sense, Papa said. Mama said she could take care of herself. As long as he made the place fit for the family to live in she would put up with him.

Papa said, almost angrily, maybe she better tell Mr. Rejenkins that her husband would do any fixing there was to be done on this house. Mama asked Papa when did he think he was going to have time to do any fixing? And what did Papa think Mr. Rejenkins was going to try when she had the younguns with her all day long? Papa said younguns won't going to stop a man that size from doing anything he took a notion to do.

Mama said, fat as Mr. Rejenkins was, Papa might not be able to stop him either.

She meant nothing by it. But Papa looked at his arm. Quietly he said, "I can sure before God protect what belongs to me."

He finished his breakfast and went to work. Mama listened to the truck drive away and sipped a cup of coffee. Afterward she stood at the window looking at nothing while cars passed one by one on the road.

One cold day not long afterwards, Amy Kay and you played in the high weeds behind one of the sheds close to the house. The two of you made houses out of sticks, laughing when you finished one all the way to the roof and the wind sent it flying. The winter wind ran strong across the barren fields, tossing Amy's dark hair in whips. You both played there for hours, happy in the cold; till late in the day Amy said, "Uh-oh. Look back there. It's Mr. Fatjenkins and he's headed over here."

He rumbled toward you in his coats and sweaters, breathing vapor, calling "Hey little children! Where's your Mama this morning?"

"She's in the house washing clothes," Amy said.

"What's your name, little girl?" he asked, petting her head.

"Her name is Amy Kay," you said.

"That's a pretty name, ain't it?" His smile creased skin back to his ears. "Are you her little brother?"

"His name is Daniel Nicholas," Amy said. "You better not mess with him, either. He bleeds."

Mr. Rejenkins considered you with a thoughtful look. "Yes, I believe your Mama said something about that to me. You have a very pretty Mama. Don't you think so?"

"We know our Mama is pretty," Amy said, "we don't need anybody to tell us so. Come on Daniel. Mama wants us to come back to the house, I can tell." She took your hand and you both walked away from the fat man, who watched the ground where you had stood as contentedly as if you were still there. On the way to the house, you said, "Mr. Rejenkins sure stinks, don't he?"

Amy Kay shook her head so fast her hair whipped out straight, and she ran ahead of you to the house, banging the door closed behind her.

That was in January, when Papa was busiest at work. In cold weather Papa stayed on the job till late at night, fixing people's broken-down furnaces and delivering bottled gas to their houses. Sometimes he didn't come home till long after midnight. You children liked those nights. When Papa was away from the house you didn't need to be so quiet, and you didn't wonder if he had whiskey in his truck or if he was going to get mad at something Mama said and start to yell at her. At night that January you slept under warm mounds of blankets, and Allen let you lie against his back. But Mama walked the floor after you children went to bed, cold because the whole house was cold, afraid because so many windows surrounded her. There were no neighbors except the Rejenkinses whose lights she could see across the fields. For Mama, who had always lived in other people's houses, the sight of that house did not make her less lonely. In her womb the new child was growing and still she had not told Papa. The fear of what Papa would say about another baby multiplied the vague night fears that haunted the quiet winter evenings as she paced the floor back and forth, back and forth. One night that January when Papa worked till long after dark, when all you children were asleep and the television was silent, Mama began her usual nervous walk. But that night a soft tap like a finger sounded at one of the windows.

She stood perfectly still and listened. When she heard the tap a second time, she picked up a knife from the dish drainer. There was no phone to call the police with, and no place to go for help except outside. The tapping went on for a long time, traveling from window to window. Later she said she thought she would lose her mind before Papa's truck drove into the yard and the sound stopped.

The noise of the truck woke you, the clanging of chains against the truck gate and the creaking door opening and closing. Papa whistled, walking to the house. You knew from the way he whistled he had been drinking. He found Mama in the kitchen with the knife in her hands, embracing her own arms for warmth. Later she said she wanted nothing in the world but to run to Papa and tell him about the sound at the window, and let him hold her close and make her feel safe. Then she saw he was drunk.

She accused him of tapping on the windows himself, to frighten her.

He shook his head. That night he had come home

happy, and answered Mama's accusations in a voice sweet to the brim. "No honey, I've been down to the pool hall with Joe and Fish playing some pool and listening to the juke box. Is something wrong?"

She told him what had happened and she walked to the kitchen window, his heavy footsteps resounding through all the rooms. All the happiness drained out of his voice. "That goddamn fat son of a bitch. Did you let him in this house?"

"I don't know who it was, Bobjay, it was just a tapping."

He slammed his fist on the sink, rattling cups and saucers. "What business does he have messing around this house at night?"

Mama said, "I don't know who it was, Bobjay, I didn't see him. Nobody asked him to come over here tapping on windows."

"Nobody didn't let him in the house every morning for the last month? Fix this here Mr. Rejenkins, fix that there Mr. Rejenkins, all nice and pretty."

"The house had to have some work done on it."

"Some work must have got done on it, all right. Oh I can see how the land lays between him and you. How many times has he been over to see you when I won't home at night? What did he do that made you pull a knife on him?"

"Bobjay, don't talk so stupid! I wouldn't have anything to do with that fat ugly thing. You talk like I'm a whore."

The shouting woke Amy Kay and Allen soon. They sat with blankets heaped across their knees. Amy whispered, "Here we go again."

"I want to go back to sleep," Allen said.

Amy answered, "Tell Papa to be quiet because he's keeping you awake and see what you get."

They hushed as the argument swelled, Papa's voice ringing against the walls. "You better not be lying to me, you bitch."

"Somebody was tapping on the window, Bobjay. If I was going to let him in why would he bother to do that?"

"Maybe it was a signal. Maybe you had it all planned so he would know I won't home."

"All he had to do was look for your truck to know you weren't home. Whoever it was tapped a few times on one window, and then tapped a few times on another one. I don't know who it was."

"Slack-bellied fat-assed wall-eyed yellow-toothed mangy stinking son of a bitch," Papa said.

"It could of been a tramp walked here from the highway for all I know," Mama said. "It could have been somebody who walked here from the back roads. Anybody around here knows I'm alone with the younguns almost every night. Anybody could see your truck won't in the yard. This house is built so flimsy."

"You wouldn't have cared who it was, would you?" Papa said. "You wouldn't have minded if it wasn't old Mr. Rejenkins, would you?"

"You talk about me like I'm the lowest trash on earth."

"You nearbout are, baby," Papa said. "Like the rest of your family."

Mama said, "I'm your wife."

Papa said, "Maybe not for long."

"What does that mean?" Mama asked softly.

"Maybe you better wait and see."

"Go ask him, he's probably been in bed next to his wife the whole time."

Papa said flatly, "I'll find out everything I need to know from that fat son of a bitch."

Mama's voice rose in pitch. "What are you going in that drawer for?"

"You got a knife. Why can't I have one?"

"Please Bobjay, don't do that. Put that knife down. I told you the truth, what makes you so sure—"

"You been giving him a show ever since we moved in this house. Well, he's had the last show he's going to get from my wife."

You heard the kitchen door close. A moment later you heard him laughing across the yard.

In the other room Mama paced and whispered. You could not tell if she were praying or crying or singing, but you wanted to go to her and maybe you would have, except a moment later she came into your room wiping her eyes. All of you gathered at her side quick as lightning. Her gaze swept you. In her hand she held a grocery bag. "Get dressed," she said. "Amy, when you're done get you and the boys one change of clothes each and put them in this bag."

Amy nodded, wide-eyed, and slid through the shadows of the room to find her clothes. She was dressed and stuffing shirts and socks into the brown bag before you had even pulled on your pants. Allen dressed himself except his shoelaces, which you tied for him. Mama smoothed Duck's soft hair and whispered in his ear. Even then, in the dark, Duck had Papa's face. She let him stand next to her, clutching her skirt while she counted the money in her wallet and found the ignition key on her key ring. "Is Papa going to hurt Mr. Rejenkins?" Allen asked.

"Your Papa is too scared to hurt anybody but us," Mama said. "Get your coats on and get in the car."

Amy Kay carried the bag to the door, giving you a tight-lipped smile. You took Allen's hand and followed after. Mama carried Duck, not looking at his face or at any of the rest of you, only watching the windows. In the living room she shut off the gas heater. You and Allen followed Amy down the porch steps into the night. In the back yard the car shone in moonlight. Frost veined the hood and the windows. Mama scraped the windshield clear with quick strokes and slid behind the steering wheel, Duck draped calmly against her shoulder eating his thumb. Once in the car Amy took him, slipping a pacifier in his mouth and wiping his thumb dry on a towel from the grocery bag. Mama said, "Lock your doors."

Four locks clicked down, cold to the touch.

Mama turned the car key. The engine coughed, tried to speak, and died. She pinched her lips and tried again. The engine turned over and over. Mama pumped the accelerator once with her foot. The engine groaned and strained until Mama's taut fingers let go of the key. She sat back against the seat and took a deep breath. Amy said, "He's fixed the car so it won't run."

Mama said nothing. Allen leaned against you and you whispered, "It's going to be all right, it just got cold, it'll start in a minute." In the starlight you watched the glistening pattern of frost. Mama laid her head against the cold steering wheel, whispering, "Oh Lord please, let it start this time. Please."

Amy sat up straight and leaned toward the windshield. "I see Papa next to the barn," she said.

She pointed out where he stood, a lighter shadow than the rest. As you watched transfixed he lit a cigarette, flinging the bright match into the dirt. In his hand metal glinted. He walked away from the barn, pausing in the clearing to face the car directly, legs spread apart. Mama gripped the steering wheel, her lips a taut white line. She tried to start the car again, not frantic, every motion calm and quick. The engine merely groaned. Papa ducked under the clothesline, kicking Allen's plastic tractor out of the way. Allen whispered soft and high, "My toy," and slid against your side. Papa came closer and closer. Mama turned the steering wheel back and forth, hissing, "Start! Why don't you start!"

Papa tapped the butcher knife on the hood of the car.

"What's the matter honey?" His voice, muffled by the windshield, oozed concern. "Is this old car giving my baby some trouble? If you get out I'll start it for you."

Mama dropped her hands to the seat, as if the steering wheel had become too hot to touch.

Papa said, "Come on out, honey. I'll get it started for you and let you back in as soon as I'm done. Then you can go and see your Mama. Ain't that where you're going, to see your old fat-ass Mama?"

Mama shook her head slowly, clutching handfuls of her own dark curls. "You younguns make sure these doors are locked."

"It'll be so quick to finish," Papa said, flipping the knife on the car hood. "You won't even have a chance to get cold."

"He can't hurt us, can he, Mama?" Allen whispered.

Mama shook her head. "No, son. Just sit still."

Papa said, "You know I'll come in there if you don't come out here."

"He can't get in here, can he?" Allen asked.

Amy said, "Be quiet, Allen."

Papa smiled. "All right baby. You had your chance."

He climbed onto the hood, the car bucking with his weight. Mama made a strangled sound. With his raw fist Papa pounded the windshield, Mama watching motionless, pulling the handfuls of hair tighter and tighter. Papa cussed and lifted the knife, slamming it butt-first against the glass.

When the first starlike cracks shot through the glass

Mama began to moan, turning the ignition key again and again, pounding the accelerator. The windshield sagged inward over her face. She watched it descending as if she did not know what it was. But at last she said, "Open your doors and run. Now."

Four locks clicked up, four doors opened. Mama gathered Duck to her breast.

She ran toward the fields, where the darkness might hide her. Allen ran another way, toward the barn where Papa had stood; and Amy Kay took yet another direction, back to the house, scooting quick as a cockroach under the back porch, hiding behind one of the brick underpinnings. You ran too, Danny, a wild circling path around the outhouse and the rusted tractor, something beating down on your brain like the thuds of a hammer. Across the yard you saw Mama, her white coat shining, stopped beside a ditch too wide to jump across. She held Duck tight to her bosom, but didn't look down at him—she watched the stars, and as Papa approached her she cried a pure tearing cry that rose out of the black earth and rushed straight through her. Papa walked toward her, laughing, seeing she was too frightened now even to think of running. He swung the knife carelessly. You ran toward her hollering for him to leave her alone, and across the wide yard Allen did the same. You could hear his small voice crying for his Mama to get away. You stretched every bone in you to run faster, across frosted grass you could hardly see for the wetness the wind stung from your eyes. Even then you heard some voice telling you to be careful, not to run in the dark where you couldn't see the places your feet were falling.

You felt the fall when it began and knew perfectly what it was. You saw the ground burst toward you, feeling nothing but calm surprise. The jolt ran through your whole body. Your mouth, open, slammed shut. Your teeth gouged your tongue.

A warm lightness filled your mouth. You lifted your hands to catch what was still falling: a film of wetness dropping dark over your hands, thick and warm. You closed your eyes as if to listen to the bleeding.

Only a few feet away you saw Papa still walking toward Mama, Mama still crying, Papa pouring out words you couldn't quite hear, and lifting the silver knife. Mama turned to the side to shield Duck, who watched the knife rise. You couldn't see them clearly but you ran toward them after that, lifting your darkened hands, shaking the wetness off and feeling the spread of heat on your chin and neck.

You circled them and stepped between them. You turned to Mama and said, in a voice altered by the blood, "Something happened on the grass—"

She screamed something and Papa spun you around by the shoulder, the bright knife flashing close to your ear. The sight of the blood already on your face seeped slowly into him, shifting anger toward confusion. He shuddered, stepped back, and threw the knife to the ground. By then Mama had seen it too.

She took a deep breath that seemed to calm the very

air. Wordlessly she handed Duck to Papa, who took the child without protest. She knelt in front of you and said calmly, "There's blood all over your good shirt. Did your Papa do this?"

"I slipped on the grass," you said. "I bit my tongue."

For a moment she simply stared at the blood. Then she gave your Papa one look full of disgust. She took you to the house. In the kitchen she laid you on the couch, bringing wet towels to catch the blood. You heard her call the others from the kitchen door. You watched the ceiling, where a pattern of brown spots formed a good man's face, warm and kind. When Mama came back you tried to say you were sorry, but she motioned for you not to talk. She paced the kitchen, hugging herself.

After that you heard voices and studied the face in the ceiling. Amy Kay leaned over you and asked, "Did Papa do that? Mama won't tell anybody what happened and I'm about to lose my mind."

Allen, timid, touched your chin where the warm blood pooled. Papa, a benevolent smile on his face, leaned over you still holding Duck, who pushed at his chest with baby fists. "You lay still and you'll be all right," Papa said. "Hold real still. That'll make it stop. Okay?"

Mama laughed in the background. "Like you can make it happen by saying so. He bit his tongue almost in two."

Papa watched the loose sleeve dangling over the piece of arm. "What are we going to do?"

Mama said quietly, "First you're going to give me that

baby. Then you're going to bed and you're going to sleep until I wake you up. You've finished all the yelling you're going to do for one night."

"You're riding high and mighty now, ain't you, Miss Priss."

"He won't stop bleeding laying on that couch, Bob-jay. He may have to go to the hospital."

You could hear Duck beginning to cry somewhere, and then Mama talking softly in his ear. To Papa she said, "Go to sleep. If it don't stop in a little while, I'll call."

"Don't you want me to stay here?"

She turned to the sink. "Right now I can hardly stand the sight of you."

Papa shuffled out of the room, the loose sleeve dangling back and forth. Mama took a deep breath and wet another towel.

Soon after, she put the others to bed too, and turned off all the lights except the one in the next room that overflowed the doorway into the kitchen, pale and soft. Mama tiptoed through the rooms, hardly breathing. She changed red towels for white ones. "I think it's slowed some," she said, wringing the towels into an enameled pan. She brought more pillows to prop your head, saying, "Let the blood run into the towels Danny, don't try to swallow it. Blood will make you sick." She touched your forehead with smooth, cool hands. "It's the devil," she said, smiling. "The devil makes the blood run out even when you lay as still as you can. You can't help it. Don't lay there worrying."

You slept for a while, or dozed. At the end of it someone touched you, and for a moment before you opened your eyes you dreamed it was a new face, something you thought you should recognize. You woke to Mama's warm smile, her gentle fingers on your lips. You rose up and tried to tell her the dream, but your lips felt sticky and wet. "Hold still," she said.

Papa sat at the kitchen table, picking his teeth with a broom straw, staring vacantly into the black windows and the faceless night. He wore his good coat with the sleeve Mama had hemmed. As Mama turned he said, "I don't want to owe no favors to Mr. Rejenkins. I'll carry the youngun on my back before I'll ask that son of a bitch for anything."

"That's fine for talk," Mama said, "but your son is bleeding real blood, and we have to do something to get him to a doctor."

"Why can't he ride in my truck?"

"He needs to lay down. It slows the bleeding."

"He can lay his head on your lap."

"That's fine for his head, but where is the rest of him going to lay? The seat's full of tools. You want to move them?"

"You got to have things luxurious even to carry a youngun to the hospital." The straw trembled in his fingers. "You beat all I ever seen."

Mama walked to the window, pushing aside the plastic curtains. Moonlight shone along her arms. "I guess you're ashamed to tell anybody you busted out the windshield of your own car and can't drive your boy to the hospital."

Papa stood, slamming the chair under the table. "Have you already forgot the tapping you were so damn scared of? You think it was really some nigger heard the fame of your beauty and walked here all the way from the backstreets to see you? And now you want me to ask that bastard for his car?"

Mama flushed red to her ears. "I haven't forgot a thing. But I look over on that couch and see my youngun's blood falling into a towel and I understand I haven't got time to worry about a fool who wants to look at some-body in a window or the fool that caused him to fall in the grass, either one."

"The youngun ain't dead yet. The bleeding could stop any minute."

Mama glared at him. "You know what his blood is. It doesn't stop bleeding. He was born that way, he can't help it."

"Whose fault is it he was born that way?"

She came to the couch and looked down at you for a long time. Presently she said, "I've got to change your clothes, Danny. We're going to ride to the doctor."

"You ain't got no answer to that, have you? You know whose fault it is."

Mama rubbed your forehead with her cool hand. "If you won't ask for the car, I will. I don't have to talk to that man, I'll ask his wife. I don't have any intention of sitting in this room watching this youngun bleed to death."

Wordlessly she bathed you, lifting you gingerly to change your shirt, pulling on clean pants without disturbing the system of towels where the blood collected. Papa picked his teeth. He drew a glass of water at the sink; you could hear every swallow as he drained it. Mama took your dirty clothes away. Papa turned to you, the black window framing his face. He pulled the coat together and buttoned it with the one hand. At the back door he stopped. "Tell your Mama to finish getting you ready as quick as she can. I'll be back in a little bit."

But when Mama came back you didn't have to say anything at all. She nodded at the empty room, smiling softly.

You dozed again in the near-silence that followed, hearing only Mama's soft footfalls and her quiet gathering of clothes into a paper bag, some for her and some for you. She ran water to bathe her face after pulling the curtains closed. You drifted in and out of a cloud, watching her sometimes and forgetting her others, aware mostly of the light and the warm trickle from your tongue to the soft towels. Once you heard her hum a hymn from church. She never liked to sing but she would sometimes hum a tune.

Later, you never knew how long, Papa came back. He brought Mrs. Rejenkins with him, fresh from sleep, her silver hair screwed onto pink plastic rollers. She wore pink fur bedroom shoes and a pink quilted housecoat that descended from her shoulders like the sides of a pyramid. Her broad face glowed red and ruddy; her broad hands showed knobby, sharp-backed bones. These were the hands that polished Mr. Rejenkins' shoes. Mrs. Rejenkins ran across the room and hugged Mama close. "Poor baby! When Bobjay told me what happened I had to rush right over here. You must be scared to death."

Mama stiffened when the woman touched her, and slowly backed away. "I thank you for the trouble," she said, "but there wasn't any need for you to bother yourself."

"Bother? Lord knows, you're the one with trouble. I'd be a poor Christian if I didn't do whatever I could to help." Mrs. Rejenkins tilted her hair curlers in various directions as she spoke. "Imagine the foolishness of it. Bobjay told me what happened. It's a wonder that child didn't kill himself on that windshield—"

"Windshield?"

Papa gave Mama a warning look. He said slowly, "It's a crazy thing to happen, him falling like that."

Mrs. Rejenkins glanced at you sorrowfully. "Poor little thing. I guess it's no need to holler at you now, is it? You're being punished enough. You won't go climbing on no more frosty car hoods, will you? It's a lucky thing you hit it with the back of your head and not the front, or else God knows how hurt you'd be right now. Likely you'd have broke your nose to boot."

"He can't talk," Mama said. "He ought not to move his tongue."

"Oh honey, don't I know!" Mrs. Rejenkins said. "Look at that blood."

"The car's running," Papa said. "We ought to go."

Mama rubbed her bare arms. "I got to wake up the other younguns first."

Mrs. Rejenkins said, "Now you let them younguns sleep, Ellen. As soon as Bobjay told me what happened I says to him, 'Bobjay, who's gonna look out for them other babies you got while you go to the hospital?' Ain't that what I said, Bobjay? He acted foolish then, like he hadn't even thought of it, which don't surprise me, because men never do think practical when there's trouble. I says to myself, them younguns will worry that poor woman to death in that hospital, and lord knows she don't need any more worry. So I thinks to myself, why can't I go over there and sit up with them? My husband sleeps like a hog in the mud, he don't care if anybody is next to him or not. We ain't got us no little babies, so I'd love to take care of them."

Mama thanked Mrs. Rejenkins and told Papa, "Carry him careful. Can you walk steady enough?"

"My husband loves your little children," Mrs. Rejenkins said. "He loves to come over here and see them. Did you know that? That's why he does all these little repairs himself, when he's got the money to hire some trash to do it if he wanted to. It wouldn't cost much of anything, there being so much trash around without work, and this house being so old."

She stopped talking and blinked at Mama slowly, exactly the way a cow blinks, chewing grass. Mama told her where the cereal was for Allen's breakfast and showed her Duck's bottles and wrote down the time Amy needed to get up to catch the school bus. Papa looked down at you then, Danny, and laid his heavy hand on your forehead. The rough, stiff skin felt strangely pleasant. "You'll be all right," he said. "We'll get you to the doctor real fast."

He knelt, and you leaned onto his firm shoulder. He smelled of kerosene and sweat and afterwards of your blood, since in walking he jogged the towels this way and that, spilling the dark stuff on his shirt. When he lay you down on the car seat he wiped the back of his neck, muttering.

At the hospital Papa parked under a rectangle of gray concrete with the name of the hospital in raised letters on the front. Papa lifted you from the car into harsh fluorescent light. As you settled against his sweaty shirt you could feel his heart pound. Mama followed close this time, holding the towel to catch the blood and brushing your hair back from your eyes. "There's not a thing to be afraid of," she said. "It's a hospital and they can help you here. You been to one before even if you don't remember it."

Papa paused at the gray metal door, a cool glaze on his eyes. Mama watched him. Papa coughed and spat. "I don't like the way this place smells."

"It won't be so bad once you get inside. Don't let it worry you."

He shook his head, half turning away. "I don't think I can stand it, Ellen."

Mama watched him silently. A softness stole across her face, that she tried to suppress. She reached a hand to brush Papa's stubbled cheek. At the touch he drew back, as if struck. Something in her tenderness startled him. Only after a moment did he lean into her hand. "Funny," he said slowly, "how this door makes me remember things."

"You don't have to come inside if you don't want to. You can wait in the car."

He shook his head, still watching her, doubtful of her tenderness. With his piece of arm he pushed open the door.

Inside a nurse asked, "Are you the people with the hemophiliac? A lady called to say you were on your way." The nurse leaned close to your mouth, as if she expected to find the blood a different color. The wings of her white cap brushed your cheek. In the warm corridor you felt sleepy and heavy. You watched two painted girls with caps pinned to mountains of teased hair writing in charts by the light of goose-necked lamps. You yawned in the nurse's face and she took a quick step back.

They carried you to a room where a little black boy slept on a large metal bed, tubes descending into his thin arms and plunging into his nostrils. You lay on a bed like his beside the window. The mattress felt different from any mattress you'd ever slept on before, as if each part of it knew exactly how much each part of you would weigh. Mama tucked the sheet under you chin and smiled. "Now you don't have a thing to do except lay there and stop bleeding. You think you can do that for your Mama?"

At the foot of the bed you heard Papa whisper to the nurse about insurance. The nurse said wanly that she really didn't have anything to do with the financial part of the hospital. But she was sure arrangements would be made when the time came.

A doctor shone a light in your mouth, talking to you quietly about a little boy like you at home, who had a red plastic firetruck and a G.I. Joe doll. A nurse wheeled in a creaking steel rack with a swaying sack of blood at its top. She rubbed the back of your hand with alcohol. The doctor touched the small blue veins with the tip of his finger. He tied a rubber hose around your wrist. The nurse said, "What a quiet little boy. Most little boys don't like it when we do this." The doctor told her that big boys like you didn't get scared at the sight of a teeny tiny needle. When the nurse tore the needle from its sterile wrap, Mama said, "Be real still now. It'll sting a little."

You watched the steel shaft. It bit your vein, sliding inside stiff and cold. From the swinging sack the red blood dropped into your arm.

After that you slept. But all night behind your sleep you heard Papa talking to Mama in a low voice you couldn't quite understand. Mama's answers were sometimes clear. "You got to work, Bobjay. Me and the youngun both know that. Nobody expects you to stay . . . I'm sorry you won't get any sleep. You should have thought of that before you decided it was such a good night to have a fight . . . That boy is not going to bother Danny and neither is his Mama . . . It was a strange lie you decided to tell Mrs. Rejenkins, when any fool would know a fall that hard would split his skull wide open and not do half the damage to the wind-shield . . ."

Every time you woke Mama stroked your forehead to keep you still, while the nurses changed the bottles of blood. Once you saw Mama walking Papa out of the room, Papa saying, "I smell blood every place I go, even in the cafeteria."

"You got to go to work. I don't want to hear about the smell any more, or else I'll be smelling it all day myself."

You woke and slept. You sipped broth through thin straws. The nurse taped your hand to a board to keep the needle still and you watched the raw blood drop along the tube into your arm, and felt it run out your tongue into the towels. When the towels were full of blood the nurse changed them, or else Mama changed them if the nurse wasn't around. Once you woke to see Mama and the nurse holding a towel to the light. The center was completely red. The nurse said coolly, "You really can't judge from the color. The blood spreads when it soaks in. A little blood makes a big stain."

Sometimes the black boy cried at night, and his Mama couldn't always stay with him to comfort him. Those nights Mama crossed the room to stroke his forehead, telling him, "It's all right, boy. Your Mama loves you and she's coming back tomorrow, she said so, didn't she? It's all right, we're here in the room with you, nobody's going to hurt you while we're here, not with all these doctors run-ning around."

The boy drew long slow breaths and finally quieted.

Mama came back to your bed to watch the blood roll away.

Papa visited, left, returned. He spoke to you gently at the side of the bed, telling stories he hoped you'd like to hear, about crawling under some woman's house to patch a leak in her gas line and coming on a rattlesnake halfway underneath. It was shedding its skin against the cinderblock foundation. Papa crushed its head against the blocks with the heel of his work boot. Or he told you about the fight he had one Saturday night at the Marine base, when him and Ernest T. (who smoked White Owl cigars) went down to this bar where Japanese women served the drinks while black women danced on these little stages in costumes covered with sequins and embroidery. Papa said a Marine with a blue scar over his eye picked a fight with him—called him a one-armed son of a bitch and told him to get the hell away from where people had to look at him. Papa invited the man to make him leave and they stepped outside into an alley. The Marine cut Papa on the cheek with a switchblade, but Papa busted a wine bottle on the Marine's head, and when the man keeled over Papa kicked his balls flat with the same work boots that had crushed the rattlesnake's head.

Papa enjoyed stories like that, and you smiled for him in all the right places. But he seemed many miles distant when he spoke, and after a while so did all the nurses and doctors, so did the little black boy's crying, so did Mama. You only wanted to gaze ahead at the white wall opposite you, seeing only the whiteness, hearing nothing, thinking nothing, feeling only the stillness of your body every place but the torn vein where the blood oozed out. You couldn't have said it in words, but you understood then that your blood had always wanted to be free of your body, that it wanted to leave you flat and empty on this bed. No one else knew about it. They watched your moist, sticky mouth as if the thing that unfolded from it was something they had never heard of before. Only Mama understood. She knew you might be leaving. But she never cried, not once, and neither did you.

The veins in your hands closed up. The doctor moved the needle. You watched the swift scooping motion of the curved steel tip into the pale blue snake under your skin. When the nurse left you alone you touched the mound of flesh the needle raised. Mama stayed beside you day after day. Papa brought changes of clothes for her, told her stories about Amy and Allen and Duck, at home being taken care of by Mama's sister Delia. Aunt Delia sent you comic books and a tin jet with an engine that sparked and crackled whenever the landing wheels turned. Mama didn't like the loud noise it made. You set it on the table next to the bed, Mama saying, "You have to be quiet in a hospital."

You slept and woke again. Mama bent over you, parting your lips, an ugly look on her face. Behind her the first doctor talked to other, older doctors. Papa stood by the window smoking a cigarette. Mama spoke earnestly in his ear, touching the piece of arm.

You dreamed of dark rivers lined with mossy trees,

of dense undergrowth alive with small animals: monkeys with orange fur and curled tails, parrots with wings that burst like rainbow bombs in flight, deer with soft tongues and eyes like flower petals. You swam in the river, splashing water backward with your hands or upward with your feet. You dove underwater to watch the slow fish swim by, or else you swam close to the bank in the darkness beneath the arches of weeds, where the water moccasins nested.

Or else you dreamed of clouds. You dreamed you were no longer a child, you were something other, something you assigned no name but only imagined: light-boned, colored like ivory, skimming the clouds on broad white-feathered wings that flashed in the clear air. The dream had no form or story, only the rhythm, the thick beat of your wings in the solid air. Your shadow skimmed the clouds. Sometimes you flew alone drinking mouthfuls of wind, reaching forward with your wings and scooping back, the whole sky empty around you—but sometimes there were others, sometimes thousands of you, above, below, from side to side, lost in mountainous hangs of cloud, wings beating up and down, endless pulse . . .

Once during this dream you heard Papa's voice, and then Mama's answering: "I found us a new house already," Papa said. "You can quit pouting around like I brought the whole goddamn world to an end."

"I'm not pouting," Mama said. "I've got other things on my mind."

"He had it coming. No telling how he would have treated you this summer."

"Don't act like a hero," Mama said. "You did it. I don't care why. All I know is you couldn't have picked a better time to get thrown in jail, with your son lying in the hospital."

"That fat son of a bitch had it coming to him. He can shove his house and his whole goddamn farm right up his own ass."

"You're lucky he didn't press charges on you."

Papa said, in a new tone, "Delia wants to stay with you here one night."

"What will you do then? Who will you fight with that night?"

"Well if you're going to get smart, Miss Priss, maybe I'll start with that doctor friend of yours, the one you're always talking about like he's Jesus."

"He ain't nothing to me but a doctor, and if you don't know that by now I'm sorry for you."

"Maybe he don't mean nothing but you sure do blush when I talk about him."

"It's what I ought to expect from you. You never quit. It ain't enough you leave me here all day to watch this youngun bleed, and him laying here so weak he can't say a word. No, you got to make me feel nasty about the only person that talks to me the whole day . . ."

You listened, you heard everything, you knew the words meant something to them but none of it meant anything to you. Nothing reached you in the dream, where you had become the other, flying with broad wings over continents of pure white clouds, not one stain of red. You listened to them talk as if they were a dream, and the dream of the other was real, the land of red lakes bordered with silver trees, lines of slim ladies and gentlemen walking along the banks, filling the sky with the soft fogs of their voices. The dream changed and you became new things, things you never remembered afterward.

You remember a long car ride and then a new hospital with forest green walls, in a city whose name you would always remember. Mars Hill. The doctors here spoke to you often. They called you by name. "How are you this morning, Danny? Is that tongue still leaking, Danny? Don't you worry, Danny boy, we'll have it stopped soon, there's nothing to worry about."

You smiled back at them, feeling the stickiness. Their faces made you want to laugh, even Mama's. The blood kept falling, no matter what they said or did, and you were sure that even here, even in this new hospital, nothing would change. All day long you felt the blood running down your chin, away into the air, a smoke that vanished in front of you.

You slept and woke and finally did not wake, easing in and out of grayness. Sometimes you saw the shapes of faces, no longer caring to see more, feeling their presence as one feels the brush of a fly's legs. You stared into the wall behind Papa's head, over Mama's shoulder, into a place neither of them saw: a river, a gate, a long stairway; you were following someone, following music, following the bare back of a man whose face you might recognize if you could catch him and make him turn around. You hurried after him because you wanted him to give you something, you didn't know what it would be.

Mama said, "Danny if you drink this cocola your mouth will taste better."

Papa said, "If you get better I'll buy you a little guitar."

Mama said, "Don't be such a quiet little boy, talk to me."

Papa said, "He don't care, he's just going to lay there."

Mama said, "Darken the blinds again, so he can sleep."

Papa said, "It seems like if he's going to—if there's nothing we can do about it—it seems like we're going to pay a lot of money for him to lay here like this."

Mama said, "He can't help it."

"I know, you say it all the time, it's his blood, it's his goddamn blood."

"Don't talk like that in front of him. You don't know how it makes him feel."

"All I know is everything in this room has to be paid for by somebody, and I got a feeling it's going to be me."

"He's a little boy, he can't help the money."

After a while Papa said, "Well, at least we ain't going to take any more chances. We been lucky since Danny, we got two good sons. We won't have any more."

Mama's voice took on a nervous sound. "You think we're going to stop because you say so?"

"One of your fancy doctor friends can tell us what to do. There's pills you can take to keep from having babies."

"That's fine if there's not one already started," Mama said slowly. "But what if it's already too late?"

Right in front of their eyes the man's bare back retreated, so close he might have slid his hand right through the solid look of hate Papa gave Mama when he understood what she was telling him. They only saw each other and the wound in your mouth. You knew then you might have followed the man forever, might finally have caught him except, now and then, for the look in your Mama's eyes.

Mama told you, years later, about the night Papa came back to the hospital after he learned he was going to be a father again. Your bleeding had slowed. The doctors hoped a clot would form soon. Papa drove all the way to Mars Hill muttering about the baby and drinking beer. In the hospital he let Mama know everything he had thought about her since he saw her last, and picked a fight with her in front of the nurses. When he began to shout in earnest one nurse ran for doctors and orderlies. But before anyone came he lunged at Mama with a paring knife he had carried in his pocket all the way from home. Mama locked herself in the bathroom before he could reach her. Papa beat at the door with his piece of arm shouting not that he wanted to kill her but that he wanted her to come out and pay some mind to him, look at him, see him for a while.

The doctors told Mama they could put him in jail if

she wanted them to, if she would press charges. She told them no. If he were in jail, who would feed her family?

You slept through all this, a deep sleep that made Mama more afraid than before. She stood at the side of the bed all night, counting your breaths.

In the morning you woke to see them both at the window, Mama facing Papa, Papa standing with arm and piece of arm clumsily folded. Past his head you could see clouds, far above the world. The dream of the other had disappeared. Your chin was dry. You could feel the large and rubbery blood clot on your tongue.

"You should have waited to tell me till after all this was over, I couldn't take any more surprises. I'm about out of my mind."

"I already waited two months to tell you because I was afraid what you might do."

Then you called, "Mama," softly, your voice strangely thickened by the clot.

They turned and saw you, and both of them smiled. Mama pushed Papa's arm out of the way and came to you.

"See," she said, "I told you it would be all right."

In a moment Papa came too, and laid his heavy hand on top of your stomach.

A week later when the clot disappeared you could eat soft foods again, and the doctors let you go home. Mama packed your clothes into a shopping bag saying Papa was bringing Aunt Delia's car to drive you home. Not to the old house but to a new one. She acted as if the news should surprise you, and you, for your part, were never quite sure why it didn't. She told you the story in the car while you waited for Papa to sign the papers about the hospital bill. Papa broke Mr. Rejenkins jaw in a fight, Mama said, and spent the night in jail. The next day Mr. Rejenkins evicted the family from the house. The new house was nicer, Mama said, in a neat, clean yard, closer to town than the last house. That wasn't the end of the news, either. In a little while, Mama said, you were going to have a new baby sister or brother, and wouldn't that be fun?

IN THE next house, the sixth one, you lived for two years. You named that house the Light House because from a distance it looked like an old white lighthouse rising out of a sea of trees. The center of the house stood three stories tall, narrow and sheer like a tower. Mama hated this house from the beginning, despite what she told you that day in the car. There were so many stairs to climb she ran like a mountain goat from morning to night. She swore it was the stairs that brought on the early birth of your youngest brother Grove, who lay three weeks in a hospital incubator before the doctors thought him strong enough to come home. Papa fretted every day about the money wasted as peevishly as if Grove had checked himself into an expensive hotel. Mama lay in bed staring at the ceiling and keeping quiet. She laid Grove's birth certificate on the dresser next to her where she could see it all the time.

When Grove came home he lay in the crib with his eyes closed all day long, a small, dark-haired toy. Soon enough he proved to be a bleeder like you. One day a razor blade accidentally tumbled off the dresser into his playpen, and he dragged his soft arm across it. The pale flesh oozed blood hour after hour, more than you would have thought such a small body could contain. Mama and Papa drove him to the hospital in Mars Hill. Once there he bled for weeks.

He almost died, Mama said. A few months later he almost died again, of a bruise on the side from a simple fall in his crib. He passed blood into his diapers and his side swelled stiff as a melon. A few months later he almost died again when for no reason, after no fall, his knee swelled to twice its normal size, bending his leg back double.

At each accident Mama and Papa drove him to Mars Hill, where the doctors hovered over him with their needles and their bags of plasma.

At home, Mama walked from room to room, listless, watching Grove sleep, touching him carefully and turning away from the rest of you, studying the road beyond the window glass.

Papa came home drunk nearly every day. He sat in his chair by the same window where Mama watched the road. By then he had managed to buy a used television for the family, and he watched the blue images drift across the screen till he felt like sleeping. For a long time after Grove was born, Papa rested when he drank. He would answer any question Mama asked him in a flat voice, looking at her but showing no sign of feeling. If not addressed, he kept perfectly silent.

One night he brought a bottle into the house and dared Mama to get drunk with him.

Mama turned from the bottle to Grove and back to the bottle. It was summer and hot. Her face was beaded with sweat from climbing stairs. She was afraid he would fight with her if she said no. The bottle had a crow on the label, a grinning black crow sitting on the kitchen table, the naked light bulb suspended over it on a thick black cord. Mama watched the bottle for a long time, and you watched her. At last she poured the liquor into a jelly glass.

They fought again that night, the first real argument since the night in the Blood House, a fight like a storm passing through the house. To you it seemed uglier than any before it, because Papa hadn't yelled this way in such a long time, and because Mama was drunk too, and seemed like him.

In the morning both were sorry in a way you had never seen them sorry before. For the first time they became afraid of the bitterness that had taken root so deep between them. Mama held you children in her arms all at the same time, and apologized to you as seriously as if you were all adults. She swore she would never drink like that again. Of all the children only you and Amy Kay understood why she was upset. You watched each other carefully as she spoke.

Papa never said he was sorry for anything. But after that day he stopped drinking and a long calm time began. At night Papa parked his truck in the wide cool shade under the sycamores, and stepped from the truck smiling. Mama met him at the door and talked to him tenderly as she pulled off his shoes. She washed his feet to cool them and led him by the hand to the supper table. Together they tended Grove and watched him grow plump and strong against his blood, till his strength became like a sign between them. For a long time he had no bleeding at all. Neither did you.

You started school. In the morning you waited beside the mailbox for the orange school bus to take you to Potter's Lake, where you sat in the old school building watching breezes stir cobwebs in the corners. Teachers told you about numbers and alphabets. You memorized.

Duck cut his teeth and wore out his first pair of shoes. When he could walk Allen took him everywhere, teaching him about things like mud puddles and dandelions and stepping on bees without getting stung. Grove, now a year old, learned to make elaborate gurgling noises. Papa said he was singing. Papa liked to hold Grove in his lap in the evenings. Mama watched them with a smile and some tension eased in her face, making her look younger than before. She said Grove would probably start talking early and never stop, like the rest of you. She said that whatever bad people might think about her and Papa, they'd had five smart younguns, and she meant to see you all in college one day, all doctors and lawyers in fine big houses.

A picture of Amy Kay from that time survives in your piles of letters and papers, her face small, shell-pink and scrubbed, smiling a smile so fragile it seemed ready to dissolve in an instant, like frost in a blast of warm air. In her eyes is a look of waiting. Even after a year in this house, when you might have looked forward to another summer of this peace, you watched Papa carefully for signs of a change.

By then it had been more than a year since you saw Papa drunk. Amy Kay forgave him and sat on his lap in the evenings, telling him about her friends at school. Duck remembered nothing of the other houses and couldn't help it if he thought it fine to have a Papa to push him in the rope swing outside, suspended from the sycamore branch. Grove laughed in Papa's face and stuck small fingers in Papa's eyes, not caring about what had happened before he was born. Only you and Allen, in the middle, still held yourselves stiff when Papa touched you, never laughing around him, never feeling easy. Something would happen to change him back. Even Amy said that, though as far as she was concerned it didn't do a bit of good to worry about it while Papa was so much fun.

You never knew what happened to end the quiet time until many years later, when Mama told you a story about something that happened while the family lived in the Light House. Mama could tell a story richly and deeply when she wanted to, losing herself in the telling, so that all you saw in her face was the reflection of that morning years ago when a photographer stopped in front of the Light House, asking to take Mama's picture half an hour before Papa was due home for lunch.

The photographer drove a convertible sports car with square white patches on the canvas hood. Mama thought the patches looked funny when the man parked the car at the side of the road. When he got out of his car there were more patches on the elbows of the photographer's jacket—black oval patches that Mama said were there for decoration, not for covering up holes. How odd, Mama thought, that a man would put patches on his clothes because he liked the way they looked. When the photographer lifted his camera out of the car, Mama drew back from the window, thinking it was a gun. The photographer watched the house from across the road, testing the weight of the camera in his hand. He flipped a match from his finger. When she saw how he stared at the house she backed further from the window, and held the curtains closed with her hand.

The photographer walked across the road as casually as if it were his own kitchen floor, caressing the camera with both hands. At first he took pictures of the house and the trees, now and then bending one knee to the ground, or turning the camera sideways, or doing both at once. She didn't think he would come to the house, until he straightened in a particularly self-conscious way, eyeing the porch. When he stepped forward a small sense of panic overcame her. She was alone, except for Allen, Duck and Grove, who were taking naps upstairs. You and Amy were in school. Heart beating, she ran to the door, listening for his footsteps on the porch—light and sharp, not like Papa's heavy, measured tread. She didn't know why it seemed so important that he was coming to the door, except she remembered the foreign sound of his car, stopping beside her mailbox, and she remembered the dark camera and the patches for decoration on his elbows.

She opened the door only after he knocked the second time. He made an impatient humming sound that she could hear through the door. When she opened it he stopped the noise immediately, as if he hadn't really expected anyone to be home. An instant later—long enough to make it seem artificial—he smiled. "Good afternoon. I've been taking some pictures of your home and thought I'd see if anyone was here. You have a very interesting home."

"We rent it from the people up the road," Mama said.

He smiled, eyeing her thoroughly, up and down. The look made her self-conscious. She wondered if he thought she was pretty. He waved his arm elaborately in the air and she could see the patches again, a fabric like velvet. "The house looks the same whether you own it or the government owns it. I rent my house too." He pushed past her into the living room. "May I come in? Sorry, I don't have much time. My name is Frank DeCapra. I take pictures of houses like yours."

She closed the door slowly, smoothing her skirt. She watched the photographer without seeming to, while he explained that he was at work on a project for the university sociological resources center. He didn't say which university. He was taking pictures of rural people—and rural houses too, he added at the end. She nodded politely to everything he said, and when he paused she nodded to show she understood. All the while he hardly seemed to notice her; he kept busy browsing the room, the furniture, the plastic curtains at the windows. Mama found herself wondering what his house looked like inside, and whether or not it was better than this one.

He tapped his finger on the camera. Mama moved to the window. "That little car belong to you? Don't you get scared driving around in something that little?"

"I get good gas mileage," he said, lifting a glass ashtray off the couch arm, holding it to the light and setting it down again. "It's not what you drive that matters, it's the way you drive."

"A good strong wind would blow you right off the road."

"A car is much too heavy for the wind to blow around. But this car is hard to find parts for, because it came from another country."

Mama nodded pleasantly. In the kitchen she could see the clock. "My husband will be home soon. He doesn't like me to have strangers in the house, so I'll have to ask you to get all your pictures taken as quick as you can."

DeCapra circled the room, inspecting the walls. "How old is this house?"

"Forty or fifty years old. An immigrant man built it, the lady told me, and they bought it off him before he died, for next to nothing. He said he didn't want the government to get it, and he didn't have any people in this country. I can't remember what country he came from."

Mama walked to the kitchen. "I don't have a good memory for things like that."

He raised the camera to his eye.

She found herself staring into a circle of black glass and turned away from it. "Don't be pointing that thing at me."

He laughed. "It won't steal your soul, you know."

"I look like a mess this morning," Mama said.

"Not at all," he said. "In fact I'd like to take a picture of you in front of your house. That's actually why I came to the door."

"Oh I don't think I can let you do that."

"You don't think a camera can hurt you. Here, I'll let you hold it."

She shook her head. "I'm afraid I might drop it."

"Then look at it. See? It can't hurt a thing. It's a box to collect light."

"Oh, I'm not afraid of it." She turned to the window and frowned where he couldn't see her. Papa would be home soon. She didn't want him to see this man here—especially she didn't want Papa to see a man like this one, young, with both his arms intact, dressed in clothes like these and driving a car like that, with that arrogant look in his eyes. But she kept her tone bright and was conscious, as she spoke, of trying to sound a little stupid. "I don't see why you want to take my picture. I'm not pretty. The only pictures I ever see are of pretty people, like movie stars."

"I think you're pretty enough or else I wouldn't ask

to take your picture. But pictures don't really have to be of pretty people."

"They don't? But you want to take my picture because I'm pretty?" She laughed in earnest this time. "Which one is true?"

The photographer blushed. She liked him better then, the blush gave his face a softness. But he was too stubborn to laugh at himself. "They're both true," he said. "In fact, these days people look at pictures of ugly people as much as they do at pretty ones." He fumbled with a tiny dial on the camera. "Do you have a dress in a brighter color? For the picture. It's going to be full color."

"You don't listen to anybody, do you?" Mama smiled into the sink. "I never told you I'd let you take my picture."

"Hey now, that's not fair. The light's right under those trees, and I won't find another house like this one for miles and miles."

"It's me the picture would be of, so I'm entitled to say no if I want to."

"But what would it hurt to let me take your picture?"

"My hair's a mess, I haven't even washed it."

"Your hair looks fine. It looks the way a country girl's hair should look."

She smiled at his calling her a country girl as if those two words summed up everything about her. "How is a country girl's hair supposed to look?"

"Light and fluffy," he said, "and a little too wild just to hang down over your shoulders, the way city women's hair hangs down over their shoulders. You should be able to see the sunlight coming through it."

"Sounds more like chicken feathers than hair," Mama said.

"Come on now, you're being stubborn."

"I've already said no once. Saying no again is not being stubborn."

"Then I won't leave. I'll stand right here till your husband comes home. And then he'll be jealous."

She stared at him open-mouthed. He saw the expression on her face and laughed himself. "I knew that would get to you! And I'll do it too, I swear I will. But if you let me take your picture I'll be out of your way in a jiffy. As soon as you change your dress."

She studied the clock. In twenty minutes she could begin listening for the sound of Papa's truck. DeCapra went on talking, something about how pretty women were silly not to let other people enjoy their prettiness, and how all women like a man to beg to take their pictures—selfishness he called it—and she smiled again, politely, but the word "pretty" repeated caught at her throat, so that she could neither think clearly about whether she ought to say yes to DeCapra and have her picture made, or whether Bobjay would come home too soon even then, or whether anyone had ever really thought she was pretty. She tried to see herself in the window glass and in the chrome around the stove burners. DeCapra said, "If you would put on a brighter dress. Do you have a yellow one? Or maybe even orange?"

She looked away from him. "I have to fix dinner. I have a chicken thawed in the refrigerator."

"It won't take ten minutes," DeCapra said. "Chicken won't rot in ten minutes. And the picture would look so pretty, all in color, you standing in the front of the house under that tower thing. It looks like a lighthouse, I think. Do you know what a lighthouse is?"

Mama smiled. "Even my children know what a lighthouse is, Mr. DeCapra."

She walked past him to the door. He fiddled with the camera. After a moment she asked, "Will a red dress do?" He smiled and said a red dress would be fine.

Mama had a red dress, all right. You remember it from the times she wore it in the hospital, when you told her you liked it better than her other dresses because it made her look so bright. It had three big round red buttons spaced down each side. The skirt clung modestly to the knee. She put on a white blouse beneath it, zipping the dress as far as she could in the back, and flipping her hair free. She had lipstick in her purse. Twisting out the bright bar of red, she wondered if it would be too much. She touched a little to her lip. But a little wasn't enough to tell from, even when she screwed up her mouth and leaned close to the mirror. She smeared more on and pressed her lips together. With the color added, her face had a fullness it lacked otherwise, being pale. She brushed her hair with quick, vicious strokes. When she told the story she said she felt the most nervous descending from her bedroom to the second floor, where Allen, Duck and

Grove were sleeping. Allen woke at the sound of her descent, and called to her.

She crossed the little room and sat next to him on the bed. "You should be sleeping like Mama told you."

He shielded his eyes with his arm. "I heard somebody talking. Why are you all dressed up?"

Mama sat next to him. "A photographer wants to take my picture. He said he stopped because he wanted to take a picture of our house, but now he says he wants somebody to stand in front if it."

"I think this house looks funny," Allen said.

"He has a big black camera."

"Can I see it?"

"No, you have to go to sleep like Mama said. You couldn't play with the camera anyway, because it's too expensive. I can't even carry it myself, it's so heavy."

"Are we gonna move again, since he likes the house?"

Mama bent to kiss his forehead. "No, he wants to take a picture of it, he doesn't want to live in it." She stood, smoothing the skirt. "Do you like Mama's dress?"

Allen nodded sleepily, saying, "It's pretty, Mama. You look like a fire truck."

"That's not a nice thing to tell a lady she looks like."

He giggled, as if he had been clever on purpose. Mama felt better on the way downstairs. Through the open front door she saw the photographer on the porch. As soon as she joined him he said, "That color will show up nice on film."

He held a small black box in her face and clicked it

with his thumb. She drew back as if bitten. "Don't worry," he said, "I'm testing the light. I wanted some shots on the porch, but the light's not right, the trees are too close. We'll have to move down here."

He bounded down the steps, almost slipping in the rolling sycamore balls. "Careful," she said. "My younguns say those things are harder to walk on than ball bearings."

"What clever children you must have." He pointed the metal thing around and clicked it some more.

"They are pretty smart. I don't know where they got their brains from." Mama pulled back her hair in a hand, feeling the cool breeze soothe her neck. DeCapra adjusted his camera in three or four different places and looked at her through it. Watching the black circle of glass, she could imagine it was simply the image of his pupil, magnified a thousand times. She could see straight through that hole into his brain if she only had a light strong enough. He pointed the camera at her and clicked it. He rolled a roller and clicked it again. "That wasn't bad," he said. "You relax pretty good in front of a camera. Lots of people freeze up."

Only then did she realize her picture had already been taken. Though she'd heard the clicks she didn't think it could be that easy. "Could you move over to the right, next to that big tree?" he asked. "Yes, there. Now, put your foot up on that root and look off in the distance. Try to make it look like you don't know you're having your picture taken."

She obeyed tentatively, looking over the fields and wishing she had a watch so she'd know what time it was. She glanced at DeCapra to see what he was doing. "No, look away from the camera," he said. "Look out there somewhere." He swept his arm in the general direction of out there. After a moment he added, "I really like your dress. Women with dark hair look good in bright colors."

"My boy told me I look like a fire truck."

The photographer knelt in the dirt. "How many children do you have?"

"Five."

Slowly he rested his camera on his knee. "How old are you?"

She looked into the distance with a purpose now, because she didn't want to see his face. "I'm twenty-six. I've been married nine years."

When he raised the camera again, he was silent for a long time, and in the end it was she who asked, "What school do you go to?"

"Mars Hill. The university of this great state of yours. I'm in graduate school."

"My sons are going to that school. They've got a great big hospital there."

"A hospital?"

She opened her mouth to tell him why that hospital was important. But she thought better of telling him too much, remembering his other questions. "They're going to be doctors, every single one of them. That hospital must be a good place to learn how to be a doctor."

"There's lot of money in medicine," the photographer said.

"When they all get fancy and rich, they can each chip in to buy their Mama a nice house of her own and groceries every week, so when I'm old I can sit on my porch and watch the cars go by." She laughed, almost as if she had been talking to herself. "It's all the rest I'm going to get. But it'll be enough."

The photographer clicked his camera, saying nothing. Once he opened the back and dropped something in it, his fingers moving so fast she couldn't tell what he was doing. "It takes a lot of money to get a medical education, Mrs. Crell."

"Where did you get my name?"

"From the mailbox." He clicked the camera again. "I like that one, you looked mad."

She heard the sound then, far-off, down the road. "It's about time I started my dinner, Mr. DeCapra."

"I'll only be another minute or two, if you'll look out in those fields for me, or up in those clouds there."

When she heard the sound again she knew she was right. The realization came with the quiet of all bad news. Here was Papa come to find this man with her, as she had known he would. "Yes, that's the right expression," Mr. DeCapra said. "Pensive. A little worried."

As the truck spun under the trees the windshield flooded with black shadow. She couldn't see Papa's face.

The photographer, absorbed in some dial of his machine, hardly noticed. The truck motor died. Mama turned slowly, arms folded, and walked away from the tree. She wanted simply to walk to Papa and take his face in her hands, to say it's nothing, this is nothing, I do not even particularly like this man—but she only watched Papa step out of the truck, arms folded across her breasts. She knew the look on his face from across the yard.

Papa flipped a cigarette butt into the dirt, and coughed. "We got company, Ellen?"

Mr. DeCapra looked up from his camera and bounded across the yard, offering his hand. "You must be Mr. Crell." He let the camera dangle on the strap around his neck, shaking Papa's hand violently. "I'm a photographer, I come from Mars Hill—"

"You come all the way from Mars Hill to take my wife's picture?" He turned lazily to Mama. She smoothed her skirt again, wishing the red weren't so bright. "I know that's a pretty long ways to drive. We take our children to the hospital there."

"It's a real good hospital," the photographer said. "It's huge. I bet it covers half the campus."

"They'll steal every penny you have, too, to pay for them big buildings." Papa ground his heel back and forth in the dirt. "What do you take pictures for?"

"Some people in my department are putting together a book on the eastern part of the state, to try and capture your way of life. Some people think it's dying out. Your way of life, I mean." He searched Papa's face, uncomfortable, perhaps wishing he'd taken his last pictures a little faster now. At any rate, he finished lamely, "We have a grant from the government to pay for it."

"Them fools in the government will pay for anything. You going to put my wife's picture in this book?"

"Your wife and the house. The house is fascinating. I'd love to have met the man who built it."

"He was foreign." Papa broke a match out of the book to clean his teeth. "My wife don't like climbing all the stairs. She says it makes her tired."

"The stairs?"

Papa watched him for a long moment. "To the bedrooms. Me, I don't mind a few stairs. Specially not to get to a bed. How about you, Mr. Picture Taker?"

The photographer blushed. "The word is photographer, Mr. Crell. And my name is Frank DeCapra. No mister necessary."

Papa laughed, shortly. "Yeah, I hear you. Mister."

He turned to look at Mama. Years later as she told the story, the hurt from that look Papa gave her still burned in her. Not the look she expected. Not mean, not like he would slap her hands away if she tried to touch him. Just scared and hurt. He didn't look her in the eyes. He stared at each button of the dress, as if he were memorizing them.

"Mr. Crell," the photographer began.

But this time Mama interrupted. "I believe you said you had all the pictures you wanted."

"Mrs. Crell, your husband has insulted me."

"He called you Mister. I've been calling you Mister all afternoon, and you never said a word to me."

He blinked at her, as if her sudden unfriendliness were a great surprise. "You people must not see much of the world out here. One stranger in an afternoon makes you behave like you've been invaded by Yankees from all directions."

"I suppose you like men to call you Frank, and women to call you Mister Frank," Mama said. She shook her head quickly, for no reason but to free herself from Papa's gaze.

Mr. DeCapra stared at her too. "Yes," he said, "I took all the pictures I want, and now I will be happy to leave." Though he lifted the camera as if he would like to point it at them.

"Get out of here," Papa said in a low voice.

The photographer jounced away, the camera flailing his ribs. But a few yards from the car he turned and spoke, gesturing emphatically, a teacher in front of his class. "You people are quite possibly crazy! All a man wants is a few lousy pictures and you act as if he's trying to steal your whole life right out from under you. So what if I don't want to be called mister? Lots of people don't like to be called mister."

"Lots of people," Papa said, stepping forward, "don't like to be yelled at in their own yards."

Mama said as he took that step forward she saw the photographer's eyes move along the piece of arm at Papa's side. He noticed it for the first time then—she saw the change in his face—and she remembered thinking how foolish it was for a man who made his living by seeing to notice so little. He drew back as much from the sight of the arm as from Papa. When he reached the little car Papa raised his good fist in the air. "If you put one picture of my wife in your goddamn book, I'll find you and break your neck!"

DeCapra raised his camera a last time and clicked their picture into the black box around his neck. Papa bent for a rock like an angry baby, and Mama had to take his hand to keep him from throwing it. She made him look at her. Behind, she heard the little car drive away.

Into Papa's eyes she said, "You're jealous over nothing. He took my picture three times on the porch. He's a boy."

Papa frowned at her mouth, working on words he was afraid to say. She led him to the house slowly. At the door he began to whistle, a hollow sound, under his breath.

Inside, she slipped away from him to the stairs, saying, "I want to change my clothes." She could feel him watching her even on the flight of stairs he couldn't see.

She didn't know exactly when it was after that, but he started drinking again before they moved out of the Light House. Not fighting again, only drinking a little beer. But when she smelled the sweetness on his breath she knew the time of peace had ended, and she became afraid again.

SOON AFTER that you moved again, to the house you live in now, the white house in the fields by the river, where you wander by the river and dream of another life. Moving doesn't mean much to you anymore. Changing houses is like changing clothes: you shuffle the same furniture into different rooms, different patterns. This new house has a circle of doors. When Amy saw the house, that day when Mama brought all of you to it to help clean, the circle was the first thing she noticed. She stood in the doorway watching Mama scour a stain on the baseboard. "I just thought of something," Amy whispered, and she lead you from the living room to the kitchen to the back porch to the bedroom to the bathroom to the other bedroom— back to the living room where Mama still bent over the same stain. Mama straightened to look at trees shifting beyond the window. "See," Amy said. "The doors make a circle. Boy is that ever lucky."

"We can play tag in here," you said.

"You try playing tag and see what your Mama does," Mama said, dipping her cloth into the pine-scented water. "I can hear every word you say, even when you whisper."

Aloud, Amy said, "You could run around this house forever, and never get caught, Mama. Did you hear that part? The doors make a circle, and the rooms go round and round. Papa can't catch you in here."

The shadows of the branches slid up and down the floor. Mama watched them. Her face made you sad. She started to scrub again after a while. "Maybe he won't be chasing me in this house, Amy Kay. He's been so quiet for so long. He doesn't act like he wants to fight anymore."

Amy nodded dutifully. You nodded too. But Mama kept her face turned to the wall.

You moved into the Circle House at the beginning of November. You will live in it only for the one winter. But you will remember this house better than any of the ones that come after it, and in your dreams you will pass many times through the circle of doors, watching the light fall through the windows, hearing your Mama walk from room to room as if rehearsing her path.

Delia

You walk beneath the unalterable surface of clouds. Cool wind sweeps down from them, singing in the pines and scattering the cornstalks in the field.

If you turn you will see River Man at the edge of the forest, and you are sure he watches as you retreat. You even know how he stands as he watches, weight all on one brown leg. If you turn you will see him.

But you do not turn.

On the screened porch Mama has set up the green table with the curved aluminum legs, and clay pots full of ice plants thicken there, bloated with winter light. The rusting porch screen sags against the pots. You push it back into place.

The pale leaves brush your arms soft as lips.

In the bedroom you share with your brothers and with Amy Kay, the light falls through the windows at a steep slant, bright enough that you're afraid the sun has broken through the clouds, ending any hope of snow. But at the window you see the clouds have not broken, only lightened, and you ask for a wind so cold it would bring down the snow like a blast of white fire against the house and the fields.

You throw your jacket on the bed. It crumples in the middle and you can almost see yourself inside it still, lying on the bed bent and broken. You would like to lie there, turn your face to the wall and press your fists against your ears.

But this room gets no heat. From the heated room at the front of the house you hear Papa's voice.

You kneel next to the bed and lay your head against the mattress, bowed down under the sound, wishing you were anywhere, wishing this were the riverbank, wishing.

Mama's voice rises and recedes; she has gone into some other room.

Papa quiets.

Wishing Mama would pack all your clothes in a bag and march you to the car and drive you someplace where Papa could never find you.

But the car has a dead battery.

Mama, if you said that to her, would say back to you, "Where would we go? Where do we have a place?" and you wouldn't know how to answer.

You sit still by the bed knowing there is no better place for Mama to take you, and just now the floor is cold.

In the bathroom you stop to pee and wash your hands. You take a long time with your hands, rubbing the soap on each finger separately.

Your hands leave wet streaks on the towels, and the

toilet, when you pull the handle, makes a roar that shakes the room.

In Mama and Papa's bedroom you stand still. Mama has pulled the curtains and drawn the shades. In the dim cool light the room feels like underwater, the cold air chilling your skin. The bed, catercornered, juts far into the center of the room between the two tall windows. Mama makes all the beds neatly first thing in the morning, squaring the corners, puffing the pillows into mounds and smoothing every wrinkle in the bedspreads with her hands. The wooden floor is swept clean and shines.

Beyond the doorway you see the living room where Papa sits with his feet on the stool. You can see only his bare feet, white and laced with veins, and the smoke from his cigarette. Do they know you're here? Allen sits with his back to the door, though he could see you if he turned around. Does Papa know you're standing here watching the veins throb on his feet?

In the dark bedroom you feel a little comforted. The hum and whine of the television you dimly hear. You wish you could stand here and refuse to move any farther toward that room where they wait. But the something that brought you back here from the river has not left off its calling.

Mama calls, "Has Danny come back to the house yet? Was that him I heard at the back? It's too cold for that youngun to stay out there this long."

Allen answers softly that he ain't seen you.

Papa coughs. The bare feet stir.

You swallow and walk into the room. "I'm here, Mama," you say in a voice so soft it hardly seems to reach to the walls. Papa glances at you and glances away. He cleans under a fingernail with his teeth, watching the window. Around him like a sweet-smelling fog hangs the scent of open whiskey bottles.

Mama asks, "Did you hang up your coat? If it's laying on that bed when I go back there somebody is going to learn something."

"I'll go hang it up in a minute," you say quietly.

Everyone is here in the living room, where the heater hisses, blue fire dancing in the gas jets.

Papa glares at you and says, "Close that goddamn door. You're letting all the heat out." The flat, dulled look in his eyes tells you he has been drinking a long time. You close the door without a word.

The television makes noises that don't register in your brain, but Papa watches it as if he understood everything. "It's a good movie, Danny," Allen says softly, and gives you a look that makes you want to be close to him. You find a place next to him on the floor, leaning against the couch. When you are close to Amy and the others you feel safe. You sit motionless and silent with them, pretending to watch the pale screen but all the while studying Papa. He bites a piece of fingernail and spits. "Spend so goddamn much money to heat this place and it cold as a bitch no matter what."

"There ain't but so much one little heater can do," Mama says.

"You so rich you want to buy another one, Miss Big Talk?"

"We might could afford one if you didn't start to spend all the extra money we got to keep yourself happy."

"Tell me about it. You earn so goddamn much yourself. How much have I spent that won't on you or your younguns?"

"You know better than me."

"You know what started me drinking. I ain't had nothing but a beer now and then, not till last week." He glares at the kitchen doorway as if she stood there, though it is only her voice.

She says softly and evenly, "Yes, I know what your excuse is."

You do not know what they are arguing about.

But Amy catches your eye and mouths the word, "Delia."

Aunt Delia came to visit last week. Papa and Mama have been arguing since she left. Though as for that you had felt the anger gathering in your Papa's silence since before you moved from the Light House.

Papa pays no mind to Amy or to you, only stares at the kitchen doorway, clenched mouth working on words he doesn't say, eyes glittering ugly so that you look away, afraid to have him catch you staring.

Amy says the word over and over to make sure you know what she means, Delia, Delia, Delia.

Mama cried because she found a thing in his truck. She thought he must have wanted her to find it because he didn't throw it away. She showed the thing to Papa and wanted to know when he used it, because it was full.

Mama said she didn't want to handle the thing again, because she had already washed her hands, but she put it on the porch and Papa could go look at it if he really didn't remember what it was.

Papa said, "You are the sneakingest bitch I ever met in my life."

Now Papa stares at the kitchen doorway with the ugly expression stiff as a mask on his face. The muscles of his jaw work back and forth. He says, "You know. You know everything, or at least you think you do. But you might get in trouble if you keep on talking."

Mama bangs a spoon against the side of a pot. "I know what I saw."

"Your eyes are hooked to a stupid mind," Papa says, "else a filthy one, to accuse me of what you accused me of."

"You want your children to know exactly what we're talking about?" Mama asks. She appears in the doorway holding a peeled potato in one hand and a stirring spoon in the other. At the bright, stern look on her face Papa quails. "Keep talking," she says. "They'll know everything then, even if I don't say a word about it, by the way you run your mouth trying to squirm your way out of it."

Weakly Papa says, "Ain't nothing for them to know."

Mama simply watches him. After a moment she says, "You want me to show them what's in the bag? They won't know what it's for but I could explain it. Tell me that's nothing, Mr. Big Stuff."

He turns back to the television. Mama moves quietly out of sight. You can hear her in the kitchen, peeling this, stirring that, running water in the sink. Any other day she would be humming a song. You can almost see the expression on her still face, set not in a frown but tense and expressionless. Nothing shows through. Her hands move deftly above the stove that has moved with you from house to house all these years. Mama is like a wall today.

Papa sits in the light from the window that falls cool and thin over his dark work clothes, over his unshaven face and bluish feet, the nails gray and ragged-edged because he does not cut them but waits till they are long enough to tear with his fingers. He turns his brown, worn face to the window and you wonder what he is thinking. You wonder whether his bare feet are cold. The piece of arm hangs at his side, sleeve tied in the clumsy knot that is all he can manage by himself. Nervously he bites first one nail and then another, though he has already chewed them to the quick.

You settle back against the couch, smelling the Thanksgiving dinner, hearing Allen beside you breathing quietly, hands knotted in the hem of his jeans. Duck sits sullen on the couch, staring into his own hands. Grove is nearly asleep with his head in Amy's lap, while Amy gazes at you, eyes wide and round.

She sticks her tongue at Papa while he looks out the window.

You nod but look away, wishing the day were over. Tomorrow Papa will have to go back to work.

As if she has heard your thoughts, Amy nods too, twirling a restless finger through Grove's tight curls.

DELIA CAME to visit after she caught her boyfriend in a shed on top of a black girl from down the road. The sight of her sweet Carl Edward scrunched over the grunting vixen tore up Delia's nerves completely; she couldn't eat a mouthful for three days and couldn't get to sleep for a week. Finally she said to herself, "Girl, you're not going to sit here and pine to death over that no-good son of a bitch Carl Edward. If he wants to rut with ever woman north of Georgia then by God he is welcome to do it." She decided she would go to visit her sister Mae Ellen, for Thanksgiving. So she sold the ring the son of a bitch had given her to a pawnbroker in Fayetteville, and used the twelve dollars the pawnbroker gave her to buy a bus ticket to Potter's Lake.

Delia was apt to do anything when a man made her angry, and men were always making Delia angry. She was a little bit of a baby, Mama said. Mama liked Delia better than any of the rest of her family, but she didn't like any of them much. At the beginning no one would have guessed there would be an argument at all. Papa was still drinking a little, but he had been in a good mood since the family moved into this new house, and Mama began to think he had forgotten about the photographer. He acted as happy to see Delia as anybody. He and Mama picked her up at the bus stop before he went to work, early one Monday morning, and the three of them drank coffee in the kitchen, telling each other stories and laughing so hard they woke you children in the back bedroom. Delia had brought three dresses with her in the brown paper sack she held in her lap, and that first afternoon she set up the ironing board in the living room and ironed all three. Only then did Mama notice one of them was the same orange sleeveless with the pleated skirt that Mama had borrowed from her sister to be married in years before. So she asked, "How in the world did you get that dress from Corrine?"

"She said she was tired of it, because it's so tight across the belly it puckers every time she sits down."

"She gave it to you?"

"She sure did."

After a while Mama said, "I got married in that dress."

"Oh I know that, she told me."

Mama walked to the window. She listened to you children playing in the yard. "She swore she'd give it to me if she ever decided to get rid of it."

"Corrine is half crazy," Delia said. "You know how she is about things like that. One day she'll promise you something and the next day she won't even remember she talked to you. I believe all that fat has settled onto her brain."

"She ought not to go back on a promise when it's a special case like that dress. She knows good and well how much I wanted it."

Delia set down the iron. She gave Mama a smile that made Mama want to slap her across the face. Delia said, "Well if you want to know the truth, Corrine told me when she give it to me that I ought not to wear it around you because it would make you mad that I had it. But even if you get mad she said she wouldn't care, because there won't no reason for her to give away a perfectly good dress to a sister she never sees more than once in a blue moon. To tell the truth most everybody in the family is mad with you because you act like you're too good to come see us nowadays, even when it hardly takes two hours to drive to our house."

"Well you're the first one to come see me in I don't know how long," Mama said. "Am I the only one that's supposed to do any traveling?"

Delia set down the iron again and shook her finger. "You know Mama don't have a car and can't but halfway get around, fat as she is."

Mama laughed. "Who told her to get that fat? It's not my fault if the fartherest she can walk is from the stove to the kitchen table. And how many cars do you see in my yard?"

"There's a car out there right now."

"With a battery dead as a cement block." Mama flung the curtains together and paced. Delia whirled the skirt around the ironing board, finishing the top before starting on the individual pleats of the skirt. "Now I'm not the one who says all this, so don't you get mad at me. Any time I want to see you I know I can get on a bus and ride. I had me a good time coming down here. And as far as the dress goes, I don't even like it that much. You can have it if you want it."

"I wouldn't take it now if Corrine and you both begged me to take it," Mama said. Though in fact she was about to cry just looking at it, it reminded her of so many things. Days when Papa had both his arms, when they first met and he seemed so tall and good-looking and kind, exactly the man to take her away from her own Papa and her own family, exactly the man to marry. "You can wear it till it rots on your back," Mama said.

Delia lifted the dress to the light. "Honey, don't be like that. You'll make me feel bad, I won't get any enjoyment out of it. It's such a pretty color."

"Orange and green are my favorites," Mama said.

"But not together!" Delia shook her head wisely.

"Be careful of the buttons. One of them was loose on it and I know that lazy Corrine never fixed it."

"I already resewed the buttons with good thread." Delia admired the dress this way and that before draping it over the ironing board again, to press the pleats one at a time. "Actually, I only want to wear it so I can get your luck with my next boyfriend. I think Bobjay is so good-looking. None of the rest of our sisters got a husband half as good as him."

Mama didn't exactly know how to answer that—she had never told her family much about Papa—and then Papa himself came home from work, slamming the back door shut and stomping his feet clean on the kitchen linoleum. Delia gave Mama a mischievous look and said, "Let's see if Bobjay remembers which dress this is."

"He won't remember it," Mama said. The sound of his

heavy tread made her nervous. When he came into the living room, his large, dark body cast a sudden gloom on her, and she was almost afraid to look up at him. But his hello was warm and happy. When she did look up, already feeling silly, she met his face descending with a light kiss. Delia giggled and said, "You two are like lovebirds! But look at this dress, Bobjay. Ain't it pretty? Do you remember when you saw it before?"

Papa reached for the dress. He carried it carefully to the window and studied it. He turned the pleats over and over in the light. "Ellen was wearing this when we got married," he said quietly. "Weren't you, Ellen?"

"I didn't think you'd remember," Mama said softly. "You never had a mind for things like that."

"How was I going to forget it when you looked so pretty?" Papa asked. "Did Corrine finally give it to you? Seemed like she was going to keep it till she busted out of it."

Delia said brightly, "She give it to me, Bobjay. It looks so pretty on me I bet I can catch me a husband in it, like Ellen did."

Papa gave Mama a questioning look. Mama explained, "Corrine wants to spite me because I don't come to visit enough. That's what she told Delia."

Papa laughed till he almost spat. "If they were any family fit to visit we'd go see them any time you wanted. But the Tote family is nothing but trash as far as I can see."

"Bobjay!" Delia said.

Mama hung her head. "He don't like my family all that much, Delia."

"Ain't nothing to like," Papa said. "Except for you and Delia they ain't nothing but a bunch of drunks and whores."

"Are you going to sit there and let him talk about your kin like that?" Delia asked.

"I don't mean you, I already told you that." Papa laid the dress on the ironing board, and came away from the window. When he sat in his chair the springs gave a groan. "You and Ellen are about the only decent ones in the bunch. I ain't faulting you."

Delia held the dress limp at her side. "Well I reckon your family must be the tip-top of society, the way you talk."

"At least my sisters all waited till they were married before they started having babies. And none of them ever screwed a nigger, that I know of."

"Hush Bobjay," Mama said. "It's nothing to start a fight about."

"I don't like you telling me to hush," Papa said.

"You can think what you want to, but they're not your people and you don't know everything about them. It don't feel good to hear somebody talk about your family like they're common."

"But they are common."

Delia made an outraged little roar and turned her back on Papa, snapping the dress like a whip. "Both of you hush now." Mama's quiet voice filled the room. "Grove has finally got to sleep and I don't want him to get waked up." She stood, looking neither at Delia nor Papa, only hugging her sweater close against her in that room that was always cold. At the window she brushed aside the plastic curtains and leaned close to the glass. "I guess I better call Amy and the boys inside. It's too cold to let them stay out so long." The look on Delia's face disturbed her. She went to the door and watched you and Allen and Amy and Duck play freeze-tag in the front yard, the dry grass like springs under your feet. Mama shivered in the open doorway. "All right you little heathens, get in the house and thaw out before you get so stiff you can't eat the supper I'm cooking."

"What are we going to eat?" Allen hollered.

"Fried chicken."

You shouted, "I get the white meat!" and everyone started to argue, laughing and chasing you, but you spun away, feeling lifted and bright in the cold. "I can have any piece of chicken I want, because I been It all afternoon."

"That's because you're the slowest runner," Amy said.

"Danny couldn't catch a fly that was stuck in the mud," Duck taunted. They laughed and you laughed, and Mama, still shivering, said, "I'm not going to come to this door one more time. Come in the house where it's warm."

She was happy to fill the house with you children, and smiled over your heads at Papa, who watched you all and said, "Don't make a whole lot of noise, younguns. I got a headache."

Only when Mama turned around did she see Delia had left the room without even unplugging the iron. She wondered if Delia had got mad and expected Mama to clean up after her; but no, even before Mama could order you all to march right back to the bedroom to hang up your coats, Delia appeared in the bedroom doorway wearing the orange dress. Mama closed the front door quietly.

"How do I look?" asked Delia, twirling in the skirt till it billowed out.

Mama nodded and smiled but couldn't find words. Papa said something she didn't hear—she was too busy noticing that Papa stared at Delia in the dress not exactly as if he were remembering it was what his wife had worn at their wedding. Delia had a larger, higher bosom than Mama, and the neckline cut to the shadow of cleavage. Delia's legs were smooth and brown, where Mama's skin was paler, and lightly freckled. "Do I look as pretty as Ellen did in it?" Delia asked.

"It's a good thing I didn't see you wearing it first, is all I got to say." Papa laughed and turned to Mama, but she wouldn't meet his eye.

"Aunt Delia is pretty but she ain't nowhere near as pretty as Mama," Amy declared hotly. "She's fatter, that's all."

At that everyone laughed and the awkwardness passed. But Mama had not failed to notice the exchange of looks between Papa and Delia. Papa watched the dress a little too long. Delia, for her part, watched Papa even longer, through eyes slightly narrowed.

IF DELIA was angry she didn't show much of it for the next two days. In the morning she and Papa sat at the kitchen table joking with each other while Mama fixed breakfast for them both. Mama kept their cups full of coffee. She said Delia and Papa chattered away like they were the best friends in the world. Delia could make anybody laugh when she wanted to. She talked as if she were in a fever, telling story after story about the Totes, till Papa's face turned positively ugly with laughter. Mama sat next to him, her hand on his large knee, sipping coffee quietly.

After Papa left, Mama washed the dishes while Delia dried them and put them away. Delia smoked cigarettes, tapping ashes into the double grocery bags that collected trash beside the refrigerator. Mama felt better with Papa at work, partly because she didn't have to worry about his mood, and partly because Delia behaved more like the sister Mama remembered when she and Mama were alone. Delia helped get you and Amy ready for school. Mama watched the careful way Delia arranged Amy's dress and the precise combing she gave your hair, understanding from both that Delia cared for you children. Afterwards Delia would offer to serve Mama breakfast, which Mama refused because Mama never ate breakfast, or she would offer to get Mama a cup of coffee, which Mama would let her do. During the course of the day she made Mama sit down and rest while she did a little of the housework.

Once she asked, "Mae Ellen, can you ever trust a man to treat you right?"

This came during a serious conversation in the afternoon, when the two of them stood at the clothesline hanging up a load of towels Mama had washed. Mama took the clothespins out of her mouth. "Nobody ever does treat you right all the time," she answered.

"But with men, it seems like the more they're supposed to be good to you, the worse they treat you. Like the way Carl acts."

"I think all men do things like that."

"Even Bobjay? Has he ever two-timed you?"

"Not that I know of." Mama pushed back hair, studying the sky, clean as her kitchen table and blue as a baby's eyes. "But I wouldn't be surprised if I found out he had."

Delia sneered. "But him and his family are so good. He'd never admit that his people would do anything trashy like run around on their wives or their husbands."

"Bobjay don't like my family. He never has and he never will."

"He don't have to talk about us like we're some kind of poison."

"I don't know why he does. But when I ask him not to say the things he says, it doesn't do any good. I've got so I don't ever mention Mama or Corrine or any of the rest. It sets him off and I can't stop him, and I can't stand what he says."

Delia absently pinned towels to the line. "Have you ever cheated on Bobjay?"

"No," Mama said, "I would never do anything like that."

"Never?"

"How could I look my younguns in the face and try to raise them to do right?"

"Sometimes Bobjay acts like he thinks you have."

When Mama asked what made her think that, she became silent, watching the line of trees across the fields, a low wind lifting her hair. After a while she said it was a feeling she got from watching him sometimes.

The conversation left Mama wondering about Delia more than ever. It crossed her mind that Papa might have told Delia the story of the photographer when they were alone. In the afternoon Delia sat in the living room gazing out the window or at the television, speaking now and then, seriously, about their mother's health, or Raeford's drinking that was getting worse every day, or about their niece Katy who was going to have a baby soon, but most often about Delia's boyfriend Carl Edward and the girl in the shed. Nothing had ever hurt her worse than that, she said. That black bitch squealing like a stuck pig, wrapping her midnight legs halfway up Carl Edward's back, him with his overalls wrapped around his knees. Delia had run to her Mama and cried. Her family was all she had in the world. She wanted to slap Papa when he said those ugly things about the Totes; it had been all she could do to keep from jumping at him from across the room. Mama said it made her angry too, but she knew better than to say too much. She knew her family had done the best they could with what they had, but Papa couldn't understand that. He had grown up a different way. If she disagreed with him it only started another argument, and God knows there had been arguments enough.

When Papa came home Delia was a different person.

Suddenly she hadn't a care in the world, she joked and laughed and told so many funny stories nobody could help but enjoy her. Mama liked it because you children were happy and tried to clown yourselves; it made you all look more like other people's children, she thought. But she didn't trust Delia's good humor. She didn't like the looks Papa gave Delia during the jokes and the stories. She especially didn't like Delia's making such a point of telling Papa what a good-looking man he was.

That night at bedtime Papa said he was glad Delia had come to visit. He hadn't enjoyed himself so much in a long time. Mama answered that she could tell that without his saying so. Papa, who had been unbuttoning his shirt, stopped and watched her. "What's that supposed to mean?"

Mama said softly, "I guess I don't really know. I guess I'm jealous. You make so much fuss about Delia. You said she looked prettier than me in my own wedding dress."

Papa declared, "I never said that!"

"I heard you with my own ears. You said if you had seen her wearing it first you'd probably have married her."

He gazed at Mama shaking his head as if she were crazy. "You and your whole family got the filthiest minds in the world."

"My family doesn't have a thing in the world to do with it," she said, and got into bed.

Papa turned out the light but didn't come to bed right away. In the darkness he stood by the window and smoked a cigarette. He ground out the butt in the windowsill and lay beside her. She waited, but he didn't touch her or speak to her. She began to feel silly and was on the point of saying she was sorry, when he cleared his throat and said coldly, "Anyway, it ain't that she looks better in that dress. It's just that I like you so much in your red one."

He fell asleep not long after. Things like that never bothered him. But Mama lay awake a long time, gazing upward into the darkness.

NEXT DAY Mama found it hard to talk to Delia at all. She caught herself watching Delia at odd moments, wondering what she was thinking, wondering why she watched Papa with that too-cool gaze. This was the Tuesday before Thanksgiving. Breakfast went much the same as before, Papa eating his scrambled eggs without a word of thanks, telling Delia a dirty joke he had heard at work the day before, grinning like a fool when Delia exclaimed that he was such a card! Papa asked Delia how long she meant to stay and Delia answered that she hadn't decided but she wouldn't miss Mama's good Thanksgiving dinner for anything, she said. Mama hid her frown behind her coffee cup, feeling ashamed of herself. But still she wished Delia were leaving today.

Amy and you were happy that morning, since this was the last day of school before Thanksgiving holiday. While eating your bowls of warm oatmeal you chattered about school, about your teachers, about the chance of snow, till Mama told you both you were probably the most ridiculous younguns she had ever heard of. She stood at the door and watched you till the orange bus picked you up. The sad look on her face stayed with you all day long.

She did her housework, Delia helping, talking quietly about this and that. Without being asked, Delia made lunch: cheese sandwiches fried in butter, and hot potato soup. The food reminded Mama of meals her mother made when she was a little girl. They talked quietly with the television buzzing in the next room. The afternoon passed slowly. Delia asked if Mama was cooking a turkey for Thanksgiving. Mama said it would have to be chicken, because turkey was too high. "We got so many bills," Mama said. "Besides, one kind of bird is as good as another."

Amy and you came home to find them in the living room, Delia with her hair in rollers, a cigarette dangling from her fingers, sending up a trail of smoke. Mama peeled potatoes, holding the pot between her knees. She watched a game show where people like her made thousands of dollars in nothing flat. Amy and Delia talked about hair rollers. Amy wanted Delia to roll her hair. "Except I won't let you do it if you roll it as tight as you did the last time. It gave me a headache for a week."

You, Danny, went into the kitchen to pour yourself a glass of cold tea, and there you found Allen and Duck eating peanut butter crackers Mama had made. You drank the tea and ate the crackers with them, till Mama came in to soak the potatoes, tussling your hair and asking, "Are you glad there's no school tomorrow? Did the teacher give you a lot of homework?"

You made a face. "She gave us this spelling stuff. We have to write this story about anything we want to, but we have to use all the spelling words for next week."

"Is that hard? Seems like to me that might be fun."

"Even if it's hard I still have to do it."

She smiled at you and said, "I'll help you think up a story. I used to be good at making up little stories when I was in school."

"We also had all this adding. But I did most of it on the school bus. And we have to read in the geography book, about this island."

"I'll fix you spaghetti this weekend," Mama said, "if you study hard. You have to be smart if you want to go to college."

"Danny's too smart for his britches," Amy hollered from the living room. "The teachers don't like it if you be too smart."

"You hush."

"You make me."

"You make me make you."

"If I'd of made you, you wouldn't be as ugly as you are."

"Both of you hush," Mama said. "You shouldn't talk mean to each other."

She sent you out to play with Allen and Duck in the yard, on the opposite side of the house from the room where Grove was sleeping. If he heard you playing he would want to go outside, and Mama said he must be still until there was no more blood in his elbow. Delia came into the kitchen and stood Amy in a chair in front of the sink to wash her hair. The sound of their laughing made Mama leave the room.

Papa came home early from work and Mama made him a cup of coffee. He sat in the kitchen to drink it, watching Delia slide bobby pins through Amy's soft, wet curls. Mama had asked him to stop at the grocery store and bring home a few things, so after a while she said to him, "You didn't get the groceries I asked you buy. We're out of salt. My dinner won't be fit to eat."

"I didn't forget," Papa said. "But I didn't come by a store on the way home, I come down river road."

"Well, I got to have that stuff."

"Don't worry me about it, let me rest a minute. I'll ride out directly and get whatever you need."

"You're going to the store?" Delia gazed at Papa holding a comb suspended in the air. "Let me go with you. I need me some shampoo and things."

"We got some shampoo," Mama said. "Don't waste your money."

"You don't have the kind I like. I need me some with condition."

Papa thumped a cigarette out of the pack and lit it. "Won't hurt to have some company."

Delia explained to Mama, "Some of the things I need you can't ask a man to buy for you." She and Papa watched each other, smiling. Mama turned to the sink. Through the window she watched the slowly contracting halo of color around the setting sun. She heard Delia say, "I ain't been away from this house in three days."

"I haven't been away from this house in two weeks," Mama said, almost quiet enough that no one heard. "Can't go nowhere. Can't get a damn battery for the car. Can't do nothing, not me."

No one answered. She ran water over the potatoes and lit the stove beneath the pot. Wiping her hands on her apron, she disappeared into the back of the house, where Grove lay sleeping on his narrow bed. She lay beside him there, face down on the quilt.

Simply breathing, she listened to the house's sudden stillness. Grove's pale face, turned toward the ceiling, made her feel sad all the way down to her bones. "His own youngun," she murmured. "His own. He don't half know you." The thought made her hurt in the belly and she didn't even know why. She doubled herself over and then, lying like that on the bed and feeling all alone, she heard the kitchen door open and footsteps, laughter, the starting of the truck. Distant. The room where she lay was lit dimly by the last of the daylight. She stood at the window to watch the truck pull away, though the windshield, washed blank and dark, prevented her from seeing their faces.

Everything inside her felt torn. She tried to explain to herself. Why shouldn't Delia go to a store with Papa? What could it hurt? Suddenly it seemed to her that things had got to that point again with Papa, that she was walking the wire again. She remembered what he had said about the red dress. She wondered if he simply didn't want to get a battery for the car, so she couldn't drive anywhere even if she wanted to. He would rather bring the groceries home himself than have to wonder where she might drive when he was away. A woman should stay home and clean her house and look after her children he said, and she added yes, you're only safe when you keep them locked away.

Now Delia. Could she be right in thinking such a thing about her own sister? Or was Mama what Papa said, a woman from a trash family with a filthy imagination? She lay on the bed and pictured Papa's truck on the highway, Delia's laughter rising over the sound of the engine.

Amy came in the room, sat on the edge of the bed and whispered, "Mama. Are you awake?"

"Yes, honey."

"Mama, Delia rolled my hair too tight again. Will you fix it?"

It cleared her head. She took a deep breath, feeling the warm child's body close to her and hearing the other child breathe softly into his pillow. She took strength from the sounds and the warmth and sat up, saying, "Let's go in the other room. We don't want to wake up Grove."

BY THE time the truck had pulled into the yard again, she had convinced herself she was only being foolish, that she ought to trust her sister better than that, even if she didn't trust her husband. She tried not to think how long they had been gone; she simply held the door open for Delia and took the grocery bag from Papa, who kissed her elaborately on the cheek. "Sit down," she said, "I've got coffee water on the stove. You too, Delia."

Papa sat. But Delia walked straight through the house to the bathroom. From rooms away Mama could hear the water running. Mama spooned coffee into Papa's cup and stirred, liking the soft chime of the spoon on the glass. But when she opened the bag, she found no salt. "You didn't get everything," she said. "There's not any salt. And no fatback either."

From the bathroom came the sound of the toilet flushing.

"There was another bag. Delia was carrying one. She must have left it in the truck."

Mama touched his face tenderly. "You're tired, aren't you? Sit still and drink your coffee. I'll go get it."

"No, let me—"

"I don't mind. I need me a little fresh air anyway."

Her sweater hung from the doorknob. She pulled it on and opened the door before Papa could move. Why did he give her such an odd look? Didn't he see she was trying to say she was sorry? On the porch she stopped to touch the soil of her potted plants. They would want water tomorrow. Swinging wide the screen, she breathed the clean November air. The cold made her smile. The truck door latch chilled her hand, and the door was hard to open but there the bag sat, on Papa's tool box, on the floor.

The seat had been cleared. Why had they cleared the seat?

Mama lifted the bag slowly, then set it down again. An odd, prescient feeling overcame her. Leaning down, with a look on her face as if she were hearing a voice, she searched under the edge of the seat.

Her heart went cold when she touched the thing. She had never really expected. . . . The feeling, when it came, was much different than she had supposed. She held the flaccid thing in her hand, still warm. She lifted it to the light. A simple sack of viscous seed. He must have wanted her to find it.

How simple it seemed. It probably had not even taken a long time.

She must not forget the groceries. Lifting them to her arm, unhurried, she walked back to the house, to the husband and the sister who was already packing her clothes; she was whispering, "Delia, Delia," and carrying the leaking thing flat on her palm in the clear air, when Papa first saw her from the kitchen window.

Delia took the bus back to Pink Hill that night. The only turkey she had for Thanksgiving came out of a vending machine in the Rocky Mount bus station.

Mother Perpetual

The smell of roasting chicken drifts through the house. Papa has sat still for a long time, but bends now to put on his shoes. He has long since learned to lace and tie them one-handed, asking no one's help. Stuffing the pack of cigarettes in his pocket, he circles the chair to the door. The thought that he might be leaving makes your breath come easier.

But when he opens the door Mama rushes into the room wiping her hands on a towel. "Going for a walk?" she asks.

"If I feel like it I will," Papa says, watching the road.

"Don't you want your coat? Or do you have something else in mind to keep you warm?"

He kicks open the screen door. "It ain't cold enough for a coat."

"No, but it's cold enough for a bottle, isn't it?"

The frown settles deeper into Papa's face, and the look in his eyes makes you afraid. "Keep it up," he says.

"You'll get what's coming to you. It's a holiday today. Ain't nobody going to tell me what I can and can't do."

"Go on then. Get out to the truck. You think I don't know where you hide your whiskey? Right behind the seat in a little brown bag."

"I know better than to think I got any secrets from you, the way you sneak around."

"Why don't you get brave and bring it to the house? I'll tell you why. Because you know I'll pour it straight down the sink. Even you can't get any more on Thanksgiving, can you?"

Papa slams the door shut behind him. You hear his fading footsteps cross the porch and descend, you hear his fading whistle. When Mama turns the anger has drained from her face. She lays her hand on Amy's shoulder and asks Grove quietly how he feels. Does he need more ice for his arm? Her voice is soft and dry as the wind through the cornstalks in the fields. All of you watch her, wanting to tell her it doesn't matter about Papa. He can drink if he wants to, you don't care. Nothing matters except that she wear some other look on her face. Amy says, "Please don't worry, Mama, we don't care about him."

"I wish it won't ever Thanksgiving so he'd have to work all the time," Allen says.

"I ain't even hungry," Duck says.

Mama turns to the kitchen, folding the towel. "I'm not hungry either. All this good food cooking and none of us will want to eat a mouthful."

You hear footsteps on the porch again. Outside, Papa hawks and spits. The sound makes you afraid, makes you hate him so much your whole body trembles, you picture him curling up in a ball and dying because you hate him so much, drying up in the heat of hate till he is small and smoking black, a dead leaf or a piece of ash, light, that the wind can lift away. But he ignores your imagination. Mama vanishes into the kitchen when she hears the doorknob turn. Papa stomps his feet on the heavy floorboards. Until he closes the door a cold wind floods the room. The flames in the gas heater dance back and forth, blown nearly to nothing. You can smell whiskey on Papa's clothes. He staggers a little, falls heavily into the chair. The look on his face is slow, stupid and thick. He fishes a cigarette out of his pocket and fumbles to light it. He flips ash to the floor. Amy glares at him full of her own hate. Softly she says, "You got an ashtray right there beside you."

When he turns to her she tries to meet his eye. He asks, thickly, 'What did you say?"

She holds herself perfectly still. Her mouth is a pinched line. "I said you got an ashtray right there. You don't have to strike ash on the floor."

Papa leans forward. "Who do you think you are, my goddamn mama?"

Amy shakes her head, flushing a little.

"Answer me you little bitch. Who do you think you are, my godamn mama?"

"Don't you cuss at my sister," Grove says, sitting up

suddenly, cradling his hurt arm under the ice. "She ain't no bitch, you are."

Papa blinks at him.

Leans forward as if he means to stand.

"I ain't taking this kind of shit."

Mama comes to the doorway, her shadow falling across the couch. Amy reaches for Mama's skirt, so angry she is trembling. "Lay back down, Grove," Mama says.

"Damn cow-eyed little bitch thinks she can stare at me like she wants to cut my throat, and then she talks to me like I'm a youngun and she's raising me—" He points a thick finger at Amy, his face distended with blood. "Say it again, bitch. Say it for your Mama, she'll be proud of you."

Amy bows her head, taking deep breaths.

"Tell me what to do again! Come on and look at me that way again, you goddamn little whore. I'm still your goddamn daddy."

"You don't act like it," Mama says evenly, stepping between them, washed white of blood. "You ought to be ashamed of yourself, scaring your own younguns half to death."

He turns to Mama now. Anger rises in his face like a red tide. "Somebody wants to fight today," he says in a low voice. "Teaching these younguns to talk to their daddy like he's a dog. Don't you stand there and try to tell me what to do like I'm nothing."

Mama answers, "I'm telling you this. When you're drinking don't you even look like you want to mess with one of my children. Do you hear me?"

"Listen to you. Don't you sound tough."

She pushes back her hair, her clear forehead blazing. "You think I'm joking? You want to be their daddy, then act like a daddy. Let them have a holiday like normal younguns, don't come home drunk and raising hell, making them so scared of you they don't know how to act."

"Who started this fight? You and your goddamn filthy mind. If your younguns are scared, it ain't nobody's fault but yours."

Mama's anger changed to contempt. She made a face like she wanted to spit. "You stinking goddamn lie. That wasn't my filthy mind I pulled out of your truck, mister. You want to see what I found again? You want me to show it to your children and tell them what it is?"

"Keep talking, little girl. You'll be sorry you ran your mouth pretty soon."

"You can't make me any sorrier than I already am."

"You're crazy like the rest of your goddamn family."

"What do you know about my family except what you want to know?"

"I know every sister you got is a whore."

"What are yours?"

"I know your fat-ass Mama fucks niggers. Hell, you're probably half nigger yourself."

"Listen to the way you talk in front of your younguns."

"Goddamn the younguns. Deny it, why don't you? I said your Mama fucks niggers. I said you're half nigger yourself."

"My Mama ain't done a thing."

"She's fucked a nigger, she's fucked a nigger. I heard your own Daddy say so. Everybody in your family fucks niggers. Delia caught her goddamn boyfriend fucking niggers."

"Delia?" Mama asks, quietly.

Papa flushes.

Mama says, "We all know about Delia, don't we?"

Papa faces the gas heater, mouth set in a sullen line. Mama laughs. "All of a sudden you don't have anything to say. My family is trash? Well what are you? Delia showed you, didn't she?"

Papa says softly, "Maybe you better get back to the kitchen and finish your goddamn Thanksgiving dinner."

"What's the matter? Don't you want to talk big some more?"

"I told you to get back to the kitchen. If you know what's good for you you'll do like I say."

"Mama, please go back," Allen whispers.

"Hush baby. He won't hurt me."

"You better listen to your son," Papa says.

Eyes flashing, Mama answers, "I'm not scared of you."

But when he stands, she steps quickly back. He laughs then, an ugly sound that rings against the walls. "Oh no, you ain't scared, are you? Look how brave you are. Why did you draw back, baby? Do you think your husband wants to hit you? I was coming to get me a little kiss."

"I know what kind of a kiss you want."

"Then come here and give it to me, sweetheart. Come on. You're the one who's not scared of anybody or anything." He laughs again, the deep laugh that tingles on your bones, and his face twists between sneer and frown. "Don't worry, precious darling. I'm not ready yet. I don't want to dirty my hands on anything as filthy as you." Carelessly he turns to the door again, stands there with his hand on the knob.

"You got to have you a drink first, is that right?" Mama circles the chair slowly. "One more drink and you'll be brave enough."

"It don't take liquor to handle you."

"Oh that makes me laugh. If you don't need it why do you run out to the truck every fifteen minutes?"

His eyes in the soft light remind you of Amy's dolls, glassy, dull and lifeless. "We'll see who talks big when I get back," he says, and slides through the open screen. Mama slams the door shut in his sneering face. Her hand pauses over the lock. "I ought to lock it," she says. "I ought to make him bust it down, or else stand out in the cold till he freezes solid."

But she draws her hand away at last. She turns, seeing nothing, hearing Duck whisper, "I hate him. I wish he was dead."

"We all wish the same thing," Amy says. "But it don't do any good."

"Nothing does any good," Mama says, shivering.

From outside drifts the faint sound of the truck door opening and closing. In his absence you breathe, breathe.

Allen says, "It ain't ever going to stop today."

Amy strokes Grove's hair. "Do you feel okay, baby?"

"I wish he would go away," Grove whispers, and Duck lies along the couch next to him, softly kissing his face. You feel their warmth around you. But it doesn't make any difference. When you lay your head back and close your eyes you want to see the river, the bending and unbending trees, you want to dream your family is dead, but you can't get your mind out of the house.

But if you can't dream any dream real enough, you can't sit still either. You don't want to be in this room when your Papa comes back inside. So you go to the kitchen to find your Mama standing over the sink.

She watches something beyond the window, something in the distant trees, and her eyes are sunken and dark. She strokes the veins of her neck with pale fingers. When she notices you, you whisper softly that you only came to get some water, and she makes room for you. You feel safe when you are close to her warmth and richness. You stretch on tiptoe to reach a jelly glass and fill it with clear water that tastes sweet and clean.

Outside the truck door bangs shut again.

"I wish he would go away," she says. "Why doesn't he leave if he hates us so much?"

You hear his footsteps in the backyard.

You hear the screen door on the back porch open and close.

You thought you were safe in the kitchen with Mama but now he is coming in the back way.

His footsteps ring on the porch.

"I hope you ain't got this door locked, baby," he calls.

Frightened, she shies away from the door, and you hurry to the far side of the room, to the dinner table.

When the back door opens you can see his swollen face past Mama's frail shoulder.

He cannot even wait to shut the door before he spits, "Now, goddamnit, do you want to slam this door in my face?"

He stands so close. Beside him on the stove Thanksgiving dinner boils and bakes, sending off its smells.

"Go in the other room and sit down, Bobjay," Mama says. "I got to finish cooking."

"Goddamn what you have to do," Papa says, stepping closer. Mama backs away. Papa says, "You still think you're going to strut around like the queen of the world and look down your nose at me and tell me what to do? No, bitch. I said slam another door in my face while I'm in here, Miss High-and-Mighty."

"I haven't bothered you. Go on in the other room."

"Are you scared now? Is the high-and-mighty bitch finally scared of something?"

"You want me to be, don't you?" She runs a hand through her hair. "Go on and sit down, you've proved what a man you are."

"No hell, I ain't done near enough yet. I want you to slam another goddamn door in my face. I want you to act like you're the goddamn man around here one more goddamn time so I can teach you what's what!"

"I got to fix dinner, Bobjay, I don't have time for this."

"Fuck dinner, you lousy bitch."

He steps closer. Mama shrinks against the freezer, her voice showing its fear at last. "Don't you want to eat?" she asks, trembling, and even though you cannot see her face you know what she watches: know she cannot, does not dare, take her eyes off the fist that hovers in the air, the one good hand Papa has. "Don't you want your dinner, Bobjay? It'll be ready in a minute if you'll go sit down."

"Don't you want to argue no more, baby? I thought you were so goddamn ready to argue you couldn't piss straight."

"I don't want to fight, I want you to leave me alone."

"Goddamn leaving you alone, you goddamn lousy bitch. Goddamn slamming a door in my face. It's about time you learned a lesson. In this house you do what I tell you!" He shouts from so close to her she couldn't run if she tried. Your brothers and Amy crowd the doorway shouting for him to stop; Mama sobs and Papa leans over her still shouting, "Goddamn you and your goddamn stinking bitch sister and goddamn these sniveling youn-guns and goddamn dinner to hell!"

She cannot stand still any more and tries to slide away from him. He has been waiting for this. She cries in dread when the hand moves toward her, and you hear the sickening noise it makes on her face. You see her head strike the refrigerator door. She cries a short sharp cry and her eyes close. He kicks her legs with the heavy boots and she crumples slowly to the floor; and then he whirls to the stove where the pots sit on the fire. He slams them across the kitchen, strewing boiling water and steam, potatoes, and beans everywhere, across Mama's face and knees, across your arms and Allen's pants. He shouts so loud you think the noise will rip him open. He turns to Mama again, who is curled in pain amid the wreckage of her dinner, but this time when he draws back his foot to kick her she rises. In her hands are the steaming potatoes whose heat she hardly feels. She slams them soft into his face and he jumps away with a cry; she might have gotten clean away from him if the same potatoes didn't trip her as she ran. By the time she regains her footing, Papa is only a moment behind.

Amy rushes to open the bedroom door. Mama dashes through it, turning to see where he is with the look of something hunted. You hear them running through the bedrooms, you barely have time to open the back door on the porch so Mama can get through ahead of him. You slam it as hard as you can against Papa's knees, and you and your brothers run into the yard; but Papa is on your heels, and gaining ground. There ahead of you, Mama has slipped again in the grass, and must stop to scrape the boiled potato from her shoe.

She is standing as Papa catches her, and he slaps her so hard it turns her head around. He knocks her to the ground and kicks her side, those ugly thick shoes against your Mama's softness, and you start to cry for her.

He kicks once, twice, and you're afraid she can't move any more from the way she hangs her head; but no, quicker than Papa's drunken reflexes she crawls under the edge of the house, on all fours like a dog.

"Now slam a door in my face, you bitch," he calls, and the sound rises thick and sharp into the bare trees and the clouds.

He turns to gape at you children in the grass, and at the look on his face you do not hesitate, you run.

You hear Amy's voice giving directions from the porch, and Papa's feet on the dry grass; you hear, too, your Mama's far-off sobbing from under the house. But that vanishes when you run to the other side of the house; you cannot hear anything from there; and then you realize that you alone came in this direction, where the house faces the silent fields and the blue line of the river, and for a moment your family is dead again, you have no family, you are an orphan facing the pines and dreaming.

But still when you close your eyes you see the twisting of your Mama's head when Papa hits her; still across your arms is the raw sting of the boiling water; and in the wind that moans over the fields you hear your Mama again, faintly, crawling in the dark under the house.

You have sat down. Your stomach hurts. You realize you are wiping your eyes over and over again on your sleeve, because unless you do you can't see.

"Get back under there!" Papa shouts, from somewhere close.

You hear Amy crying in the house.

Queenie, confused by the shouting, comes to you wagging her tail halfheartedly, unsure whether you'll pet her or not. When you don't move she pushes her wet nose into your face, and you lean against her warmth.

You hear Papa's voice coming closer. If you ran for a door he might catch you.

You hear Mama crawling, taking sharp breaths. Papa stands around the corner out of sight, snarling, "I hear you under there."

The crunch of dead grass under the dead leather boot.

You let Queenie go and then you crawl under the house, fast and light on your hands and knees, toward the sound of your Mama's breath in that darkness through spider webs and shards of glass.

You hide behind the concrete underpinning as he rounds the corner. Outside in the light a cigarette butt falls to earth, and his boot crushes it flat. You flatten yourself against the concrete blocks, as he kneels to look under the house. He is so close he can hear you breathe. He rests the good hand in the grass. You count the hairs on the back of it. "Where is she gone?" he mutters, spitting into the dirt. He leans toward the house. His shadow falls across your knee. You freeze against the blocks, heart beating in stiff bursts. It seems he will wait there forever, listening. The wind moans far overhead, through nets of bare tree branches. Far off you hear your Mama's ragged crying.

Papa spits again, stands and moves on.

You crawl slowly in the soft dirt that cakes your arms to the elbow. Careful to place your tender hands in the pure dirt, careful to watch for the glitter of glass.

You find a doll's foot, hollow and flesh-colored. You find an empty Valvoline can, a rusted lawnmower blade, an old red hunting cap with the brim chewed by rats.

Mama hardly makes a sound now. But at last you find her, a paler shadow in the light that drifts under the house's raised edge. She leans against another of the concrete supports, the blocks shielding her from the side of the house where Papa stalks her.

When she hears you crawling she gives a quick gasp and lifts something to throw.

You whisper, "It's me, Mama."

She recognizes you without relief or curiosity or even affection, with only a white look that makes you colder inside. You wonder if you should have come. The tears have dried to simple lines on her face, pale like scars. She breathes softly and watches you as if you were miles away. What you see in her eyes you don't understand, but you will remember the exact shape of the gaze as vividly always as you see it now, carried like a cold stone in your brain. She has turned her sight inward, far from you and Papa, far even from this dirt she squats in, clutching her arms.

You are frightened, you cannot move.

Her mouth forms some word you cannot hear.

"Is he still out there?" she asks hoarsely.

"Yes ma'am," you whisper.

She traces a curved line in the dirt. After a while she turns to you, and you understand she is coming back to you from somewhere, though you're not sure she wants to. "I don't know what to do," she says.

"He won't come under here. He'd get stuck if he tried."

"Am I supposed to sit here like a pig all day?" Her face clouds with anger. You answer, "No ma'am," softly. She faces you again, and with an exertion of will she sees you. "You shouldn't have come here. There's too much glass for you to be crawling around in the dark."

"I was careful."

She nods, but hardly seems to hear. Sinking back against the concrete pillar, she gazes blankly at the grayed floorboards overhead. She sets her thumb against her lips, and her eyes fill. She says the same word she said before, "Mama," she says, and when you hear it you belly grows cold. She closes her eyes and says, "Oh Mama help me"; the words send a shiver through you as she runs her teeth along the back of her palm. Her face like an open window through which light pours. When she calls for her Mama again you feel as empty as if you had never been born, and what you fear but do not understand is that she wishes that were true, is that she is calling for what she never had. You crawl closer to her, your hands and knees making tracks in the dirt.

You whisper, "Mama," to her, and she watches you. Gently and slowly you touch her arm. Only for an instant, because her skin is cool and because she gives you a look that tells you not to press for too much; as if the whole flesh is a bruise.

"I'm all right, son," she says, "don't worry."

From far off comes his voice. "Hello honey. You think

I don't see you? Well baby, even if I don't see you I know exactly what you're doing."

She signals you to be quiet and shrinks into the darkness.

"You got that dog under there, don't you?" He laughs, the sound echoing among the pillars, so you know he is on his knees leaning under the house. "You got you a dog to fuck, don't you baby? To keep you company? I saw it crawling under there."

She makes a face as if the words stink, curling her lips.

"Is it good to you, baby? I want to hear you moan."

At the edge of the house you see your brothers' knees, and Amy's too, a little distance from them, flashing as she runs to the corner of the house. She kneels and, even in the darkness, knows exactly where to find you. Gesturing to the front side of the house, she mouths words that are meant to tell you Papa stands there.

You whisper softly, "He's beside the porch."

Mama nods but presses her finger to her lips. Her hands silently rearrange the folds of her dress. She shivers. The dress has short sleeves. Her bare arms are white with the cold.

You turn to Amy and embrace yourself with your own arms, as Mama does, shivering elaborately. Then you point at Mama. After you have gone through the shivering motion again, Amy understands, and soon you hear the distant closing of the screen door.

One by one your brothers bend to look at you. Then,

suddenly, they run for another corner of the house. You whisper, "He's coming to this side, Mama, where he can see you."

"Let him," she says. "Let him come get me if he wants to, I don't care any more." But her voice barely carries as far as your ears. After a moment she moves, slowly, round the concrete pillar to the side that will hide her from him.

You see Papa's feet against the fields. "You like it under there?" he calls. "You ain't scared you'll wake up a snake under there? I bet there are lots of snakes made their nests round where you are."

She carefully smoothes her hair to lie flat against the block, to shield her face from the rough cement.

"You get your foot in a snake's nest, they'll bite you even in the dead of winter."

"Liar," she says softly, "liar, liar, liar."

"Did you put your hand in any dog shit when you were crawling around?"

She clenches her fists against her ears and shakes her head when his rough voice comes again. "You sure were a pretty sight crawling under there. Did your Mama teach you how to scoot under a house so fast? She must have raised you with the dogs. I know she used to run from her old man."

"You hush about her," Mama whispers.

"You told me how he used to take his bullwhip to her. To get the old sow moving, is what I reckon. Took a little whipping to make her fat ass do what she was supposed to do."

She makes a low sound that shivers under your skin. "Your Mama was so fat she probably didn't even feel it."

Her faces dances from expression to expression faster than you can read; though some are anger and some are hatred and during others new tears well up and fall. Too numb to back away, you watch. Once you almost call for her and touch her, but as if she can see you through closed lids she backs away against the cold flat blocks and shakes her head. You shiver. You sit in a tight ball. You know your face is wet because the wind chills your skin peculiarly, but it only hurts when she says the word again, says *Mama, Mama,* over and over; but you must not make a sound. She is strangling, she clutches the pit of her belly, and what she sees is this: her own Mama crouched against a porch while her Daddy walks slowly forward, taking his time because he knows he has his wife in a corner, with no place for her to run. He uncoils the ugly brown leather rope as her Mama begins to plead with him to stop, please stop, against the glitter in her Daddy's eyes as he makes the long whip wiggle in the dirt. When she runs he winds it round her legs and pulls her down. The whip is his power, and later your Mama would bathe the scars it cut into her Mama's flesh. The story your Papa shouts under the house is true, your Mama will tell it to you someday.

Maybe it has come to your Mama now: the knowledge that your Papa and her Daddy are the same man, that maybe the feeling your Papa first gave her was no more than that; maybe something in her made her pick

Bobjay Crell because he was like the Daddy she had known all her life, and maybe the feeling never was love.

She shudders, draws blind signs in the dirt.

Knowing her children have watched her beg as she watched her mother beg.

Maybe even that her Mama, in the last moment before the bite of the whip on her arms, cried for her Mama.

She looks at you. Suddenly she opens her arms and draws you warm against her side, her soft ribs blowing in and out, raising and lowering like wings. "It's going to be all right, isn't it?" she says, stroking your hair.

You whisper, "Yes ma'am," though you don't know and don't understand.

While Papa marches around the house, feet sinking in the grass, you move with your Mama to stay out of his sight.

Your Daddy

in Time

When Allen crawls under the house to bring Mama a sweater, she sends you away, because of the glass, she says, though she will not look you in the eye. You are bound to cut yourself in the dark if you stay, she says. You should find Grove and take care of him. Allen watches you solemnly. He whispers that Papa is hiding at the front of the house. He keeps his distance from Mama. When you turn away she does not watch you go; she whispers, "Be careful," to the air.

You crawl slowly through the litter of jagged glass. Old cobwebs drift into your hair. You set down your hand onto the doll's foot and the air whistles out. Once you look back at Mama and Allen, but their shapes are indistinct in the darkness; you can hardly tell which gray mass is which. At the edge of the house you hurry into the light. You do not see your Papa until his shadow crosses your hands.

He is drinking from the bottle, long sucking swallows that make his throat muscles slide and convulse. He squints as if the whiskey hurts going down. Only when he tears the bottle from his jaw does he see you.

You freeze. He replaces the bottle in the bag without hurry. Soon it rests in the pocket of his coat. When he reaches for you he smiles. The good hand descends onto your shoulder. As he lifts you, a pain flashes through your arm. Maybe you squirm, or maybe he is afraid you will fall because the one hand can't keep you steady. His grip on your shoulder tightens and tightens. You try to keep from looking at his face though you can smell his breath and feel the stubble of his beard. You do not make a sound. "You thought you were smarter than your Papa, but he caught you, didn't he?" He hoists you higher, till you are level with his gaze. He curls his lips. "Ain't you got nothing to say to me? You can hide with your Mama under a filthy house, but you don't even want to talk to your Papa."

He gathers you so close you squirm to get away. In his eyes you see glittering light that makes you cold. You bend back your head to escape that sweetish smell of his breath that reminds you of clotting blood.

"You hurt my shoulder," you say softly.

"I didn't mean to," he says.

"You grabbed me too hard."

"I did not. Does it still hurt?" He gives you a dull stare, stroking your shoulder with his bearded chin. He sways with your weight, once nearly falling, catching himself against the corner of the house with the piece of arm. He pulls you close and stoops to see under the house. "Where is your Mama?" he asks, but you don't answer.

Your shoulder throbs more sharply with each pulse of blood. Once you see Duck behind Papa, pointing at you and calling. Out in the fields you see Queenie nosing among the cornstalks, belly swaying like a bruise. "You wouldn't have got hurt if you hadn't tried to be smart like your Mama. It probably won't me who hurt you. You probably hurt your shoulder under that house."

"You grabbed me too hard, I felt it," you say, counting the veins in the whites of his eyes, a red lace. Papa touches you with the piece of his arm and studies you. Suddenly you think he is sad. "You don't want to talk to me, do you?" he asks.

From far off you hear Amy shouting. You shiver, bare-armed in the November wind.

"Answer me," Papa says. "You ought to like me, because I'm your Daddy. But here I been carrying you for five minutes and you ain't hardly said a word."

You feel the funny feeling in your belly that you get from the smell of whiskey. You say, "I don't like it when you yell."

"I ain't been yelling at you," Papa says.

"You been yelling at Mama all day."

He asks, in a softer voice, "Does your arm still hurt?"

You touch it with your hand. The big ache is gone, leaving only the little, underneath ache that will gather and swell against the bone. The blood leaks out of the vein where he grabbed you. But you say, "It's better now."

Queenie, at the edge of the yard now, pauses at the

sight of Papa and walks slowly toward him, wagging her tail.

"My arm hurts sometimes," Papa says. "But I don't say nothing, I don't want nobody to think I'm crazy. The doctor can't do nothing about it, because my arm's not there." He laughs. His teeth are yellow and flat. The sleeve swings idly. Queenie wags her tail and lopes forward, tongue quivering.

Softly you ask, "Does it hurt now?"

He hears you from far away. He shakes his head, not watching you, though you can see yourself in his black pupils. "It don't mean anything," he says. He nudges Queenie with his foot. "Bitch," he says, "get away." Queenie gazes up at you both, confused that no one will pet her. When she comes back he only pushes her away again, more roughly, his work boot pressing the place where her fat puppies sleep. She watches mournfully as Papa turns to the house again, stooping to search for your Mama. "There she is, at the front," he says, and runs toward her with you bouncing against the bone of his shoulder, the pain in your arm increasing

At the front of the house Papa stops beneath the sycamores that guard the house from the road. The branches darken the light falling from the gray table of clouds. The wind rushes through you, cooling even the ache. Can Papa feel the wind even in the arm that isn't there? The sleeve streams back, hangs useless against the wind, and slowly falls. When Papa has a coat on, does the arm that isn't there feel like it has a coat on? Does it feel naked? Does it hurt when another arm passes through its space?

"Has she got out already?" Papa asks.

He isn't asking you. On the porch stands Amy Kay with Grove beside her, both watching you with fear on their faces.

"You put my brother down," Amy says.

"I asked you a question. You better answer it."

"I ain't telling you nothing."

Grove whispers past his fist, "You better leave him alone," his voice so hoarse and soft the wind almost drowns it to nothing.

"Put me down," you say in Papa's ear, and when he stares at you, you rest your fists against his neck as if you can push yourself away.

Seeing the fists, he tightens his embrace till you can hardly breathe. "I'm still your Daddy," he says.

You make no sound, you hold your face perfectly still.

"You don't tell me what to do," he says, "you don't tell me to put you down."

You draw shallow breaths, you pretend the pain in your shoulder and ribs is for someone else.

"Leave him alone!" Amy shouts, and then she hollers for Mama; but you only watch Papa, pressing your fists against the veins of his neck.

Allen crawls out from under the house and runs to the porch, with Duck behind him.

They call Mama now, watching you fight to breathe,

and soon she comes out herself. Hands on hips, she watches Papa, the shadows of tree branches woven over her face.

At once Papa takes on a look of expectancy.

"Turn Danny loose," Mama says.

"I ain't hurting him," Papa answers, smiling.

"No, you're not hurting him, you're squeezing him so tight he's turning blue."

"Are you going to start your shit again, Miss High-and-Mighty?"

"I said put him down, Bobjay. He can't breathe."

He only smiles and squeezes you tighter. You dig your knuckles hard against his bones and arch your back, sipping the air since you can't drink it. Papa gives you an ugly look that passes through you, but still your expression stays the same. You stare at the vein you have gathered in your hands. You count the slow swing of the empty sleeve back and forth in the air. "Put him down," Mama says. "You hurt that youngun and I swear I'll make you sorry."

"If he gets hurt it won't be my fault. You're the one had him crawling under that house."

"Who had me crawling under there? You son of a bitch, put him down!"

Papa looks at you and laughs. "Look at his face. He ain't scared, he hates his Daddy."

You turn your face to the sky.

"Bobjay Crell, you put my youngun on the ground right now, you dirty one-armed son of a bitch."

Papa smiles a slow wide smile. "What did you call me?"

"Put him down."

"No, what did you call me? You called me a one-armed son of a bitch. I want you to call me that again."

Slowly his grip on you loosens and you slide to the earth. Your shoulder throbs and you gasp for air, you kneel in the pale grass and breathe, breathe.

Mama pushes back hair and says, "Danny, come over here now," motioning toward the porch. But Papa steps toward her and she backs away.

His face is darker than the clouds. "Go ahead and run."

"I can't run. You hurt my leg."

After a moment he laughs. "Oh boy. You're sorry you said it now, ain't you?"

"I was mad, Bobjay, I didn't mean it." She steps back. "Please leave me alone." She backs up the steps, hands reaching for support she doesn't find. There is only air, and Papa laughs, and takes a step each time she does, and says, "You can't go anywhere else, honey."

The hand rises.

A cry from the porch, Amy.

Mama makes a low sound from the belly.

"No, leave her alone," Allen says.

But the sound comes to you from such a distance, there is a hush on this grass where you are still catching up with air. Duck jumps off the porch and runs away crying, his hands on his ears. Papa is shouting something.

Mama has already fallen, and is raising her arms to cover her face. Her voice surrounds you, entering like a knife, and you feel as if you bleed from the hearing. You look away from them, at the trees swaying serenely in the wind. But even then you can picture her face when he slaps her, and the sounds she makes rise round you in spirals.

He makes her crawl into the house since she crawled under it.

Says *Don't ever call me no one-armed sonofabitch baby.*

She says *Please, please, I didn't mean it.*

While Amy says softly Mama, Mama, sags against the porch post saying Mama, and Mama disappears into the house on her hands and knees with her hair falling over her face.

The wind descends onto the house and fields, onto your face, onto Mama's vanishing skirt and legs and new bruises, descends onto the trees and the river, a noise, a rushing that almost makes you cold enough inside that you don't want to follow them into the house, that you don't want to see her after he finishes with her.

But when the door closes you stand. Their shouts are muffled by the house. You watch Allen and Amy and Grove. Allen goes to the door and opens it, and then Amy rushes inside with a strangled cry, only to run into Papa's legs.

Over you he hovers a moment, and a new cold rushes through you as he watches you. He has swept Amy to one side and Allen to the other. He gives you a long strange look. "My arm hurts now," he says, and walks to the truck. Fishing the bottle from his pocket, he drains it and throws it in the grass. He starts the truck and backs down the driveway, and clatters away down the road, between two dark banks of trees.

The Children's Altar

Smoke from Papa's cigarette swirls in the light in the place where he had stood.

When you have all come inside Amy closes and locks the door. Allen hurries toward the bedroom but stops. Mama is a motionless figure on the floor. You see a coil of white, part of her dress, then an arm, a lock of her hair, her upturned face, Allen standing beside her silent.

Seeing him, she stirs.

By then you stand next to him, and behind you is Amy, and Duck leads Grove by the hand, and you wait there, watching her rise.

A dark streak glistens under her nose. Red streaks a little place on her dress. She whispers, "You younguns go back to the living room," her voice so weak it hardly reaches you. You eye each other and stay. Breath shivering into her, she leans up on thin arms, a swirl of the smoke twining round her and light filling her hair. She says, "I don't want you to see me like this"; she chokes, coughs into her hand. At last she stands and pushes past you into the bathroom. She closes the door. Behind the rush of water down the sink you can hear her voice, a chant.

The others listen, watching each other. But you run into the living room, lie down on the couch and stuff your fist in your ears. The dark couch smells of tobacco, the upholstery scratches your face, but you press against it hard to hide from the light. You see only the colored shapes that dance against your lids when you close your eyes too tight.

Footsteps echo in the next room.

Amy says something too low to hear.

The sound of the wind rises as the water stops.

Pale shadows move on the TV screen, that no one thought to turn off when everyone went outside. It gives you an odd feeling that the people on the television shows have been moving the whole time, playing to an empty room. You go to the window, where you search the yard. Wind lifts the dry light leaves off the ground. No one walks in the fields but Queenie, a white blur nosing this way and that among the cornstalks.

"Can you hear me, stupid?" Amy asks. "Help me clean up this mess in the kitchen. You don't need to keep watch. He ain't coming back for a while."

"I was looking out at the yard," you say.

"You don't need to daydream, you need to help me." She adds in a whisper, "I don't want Mama to see the kitchen like this. I got some of it cleaned up already, but there's still snap beans all over the floor."

In the kitchen you pick up pieces of boiled bean and

potato with your fingers. Finding the mop in the pantry, you wet it and mop the floor, Amy directing you to this or that spot she says you've missed. She washes all the pots and bends them back into shape. She washes potatoes too, and starts to peel them as you rinse out the mop and put it away.

Your brothers stray into the kitchen one by one and watch the two of you. Amy sits Grove in a chair and makes him show his arm, which Duck swears is all right. He didn't hurt it again while Allen was looking after him. "It was already hurt before that," Amy says, and tells him to hush talking so loud.

They sit at the table listening to the wind rush against this almost empty house, pouring over and under and around the joined boards and making them groan, as the light pales again, the clouds thickening.

Amy drops the brown peelings in the grocery bag that is full of trash. She washes the potatoes till they're white as the skin over her knuckles.

Mama is a rustle two rooms away, a soft hiss of cloth. Soon the bedroom door opens.

Mama has brushed her hair and pulled it back tight through a red plastic barrette shaped like a butterfly. Her dress is a fresh one, white, patterned with blue flowers. She still wears the sweater Allen brought her, and stands silent over the trash bag picking out the pieces of grass caught in the yarn. She favors one leg. On her cheek a small bruise swells, and her cut lip puffs out a little. "You cleaned up real good in here," she says softly.

Amy whispers, "I turned off the oven too. The chicken didn't burn or anything."

Mama nods almost shyly, keeping the bruised side of her face in the shadow. "I knew I could count on my girl. Maybe with him gone we can eat us some dinner in peace."

"I hope he stays gone forever," Allen says.

"I hope he drives his truck off a bridge," says Duck.

"We all hope so," Amy says.

Mama only cleans her sweater, and then, nudging the trash bag with her toe, says, "That's enough mean talk. Danny, take the trash out and burn it. You boys go in the living room and straighten up in there. Amy and me got work to do."

Amy slices potatoes as Mama opens cabinet doors, handing you the book of matches. The trash is light and doesn't hurt your shoulder. Mama says, "Be careful in the wind," and you nod, while in the living room your brothers turn up the sound on the TV, and Amy, with that serious look on her face, asks Mama to teach her how to light the pilot on the stove.

OUTSIDE THE wind carries you to the trash pile and you run like you're not supposed to, picturing yourself a stream of wind over the fields, soaring above the treetops and curling into the clouds, higher and higher till you fly where the air is clean and perfect. You run under the clothesline and past the johnny house, picking your feet high off the ground like a prancing pony, imagining you make no noise running even on the dry grass. Your face streams with cold, your hands are quickly numbed, the wind cuts like knives through your sweater and shirt, so cold it tickles and you want to laugh. At the barrel where you burn the trash you fumble with the matches, sparks popping onto the backs of your hands. A small flame wavers on the edge of the bag, a blue flower. You hover over it and protect it from the wind with your hands.

In the top of the bag under the potato peels you pick out margarine wrappers and a wad of tissue that will burn fast. You lay them near the little fire. Now you become a witch and a master of fire, and this bag of trash is a city you mean to level. You stand beside it, arms folded, watching the city walls strip away under the fire, hearing the voices of the tiny people calling for mercy; but you shut your ears to their cries, you are big as a mountain compared to them, and you're angry as God when Moses struck the rock with his staff; you don't pity them for their crying. At the center of the burning you imagine your father's face, letting the flames catch hold of the edges and curl the flesh inward like this paper, till it burns him and blackens him to the eyes, which split open in the heat and spill tears over the trash, hissing like rain in the flame.

You look up at the clouds, an even sheet of gray.

You picture snowflakes falling into the fire.

The trash burns quickly. Smoke pours into the

clouds. You feel the heat on your face and lean toward it, staring down into the white heat where the bag and the cardboard have turned to ash. The city has vanished. Even the fire master can't make fire without fuel. At the end a gray shape wavers in place of the bag, that collapses when you poke it with a stick.

The wind whirls ash into your hair. The cold washes the last traces of the fire's warmth from your face. You have turned to stone in the cold. You are white like the pictures of statues you have seen at school, and smooth all over, and cool as if you are frozen. Nothing touches you or makes you feel. You don't know how long you have stood here perfectly still, and really, you might go on standing here all day, if you didn't hear the sound of a truck passing on the road. In front of the house it slows down. It sounds like Papa's truck. You run to the corner of the house.

The truck is green, not blue like Papa's. The truck is green. It passes the house.

You go back to the house without dreaming any more dreams.

THE KITCHEN windows have fogged with the heat from pots on the stove, and Amy stands on a kitchen chair learning to make brown gravy in an iron skillet. Beside her, Mama watches, sipping coffee. The coffee spoon makes a brown stain on the white of the towel where it rests.

"Did you watch till the fire was out?" Mama asks.

Amy says, "It took him long enough for that trash to burn twice."

"The fire just now went out," you say. You open a new grocery bag beside the sink. The bruise on Mama's face is larger, darker-colored, shining in the light from the window.

Even with the television playing, the house seems quiet now, and the sound of the wind outside only makes the inside seem safer and warmer. Mama locks the back door after hurrying down the porch to hook the screen. The front door is locked and bolted. Your brothers sit in a line on the couch watching the parade on TV. Duck says he bets that stuff on the floats ain't even real. Allen says be quiet and watch it. Grove sits between the two of them, cradling his arm.

"Grove's arm is hurting him worse," Amy says quietly to Mama, and Mama answers, "I expected it would."

She goes to Grove and leans over him, touching the swollen place carefully. You watch her and touch your shoulder the same way, but you say nothing.

Mama's voice, when she speaks, fills the rooms in a way that Papa's never does, loud as he shouts. Her fullness is all of warmth and softness, with no blade edge. She asks if the arm hurts bad, and Grove nods that it does. She asks if it started hurting when Papa was yelling and Grove answers that it did. Papa's chair, turned toward the television, seems to mock you.

Amy says, "My arm is tired. Come stir this for a while."

You take her place in the chair and stir with the arm that isn't hurting, though you are clumsier using it and must go slower. "Stir at the bottom so it doesn't stick," Amy says, "and stir all around so it doesn't make lumps. You better not let it make lumps, either, because I had it going real good." She sets the table, laying out flowered plates one by one. Mama has set the tea jar in the window. The smell mingles with the other smells. Soon Mama comes back to mix the tea and break ice into glasses. She has brought Grove into the kitchen, the swollen arm wrapped in an elastic bandage. Allen and Duck take their seats too, turning up the sound on the television so they can hear the parade announcers. Amy says, "I don't see what's so hot about a bunch of balloons."

Mama mashes the potatoes with milk and margarine. You throw the greasy wrapper away.

Once, when a car passes outside, everyone looks at everyone else.

Mama says, "He won't be back for a while."

She sets the bowls of food on the table, and the pan of biscuits golden on the top, and when she opens the oven door again you watch the chicken and pour tea from the jar, careful not to spill any, while Amy takes the glasses one by one to the table.

Mama says for you to sit down, that you have stirred the gravy half to death, and you find yourself smelling the food and feeling glad you don't have to eat it when Papa is here. For a moment everything seems peaceful and right.

Mama heaps everybody's plates. You see how she watches all of you, waiting to see if it makes you happy to have this— and even though you could not say it does, you understand she has worked hard, and wanted something better.

At last, because you are hungry, you eat. Mama eats too, chewing slowly because of the bruise. Your brothers tell her how good everything is, and you say the same thing, and so does Amy, and Mama smiles almost shyly. At last she says, "Well thank Amy too, because she sure helped. If she hadn't thought to turn off that oven, there wouldn't be a mouthful fit to eat."

"We'd have us this big old piece of charcoal for dinner," Duck says.

"We could of cooked one of them birds I killed at the river," Grove says.

"Did you kill a bird?" Amy asks, and Grove nods, laughing when she shivers and says, "It makes me sick to think about it."

"There wouldn't have been two mouthfuls to it," Allen says. "It was this little old sparrow."

"And him too little to lift the gun," Mama says. "Is that why your arm is bleeding again?"

He shakes his head, waving the fork at her. "No ma'am. It started when Papa was shouting. That gun didn't do nothing."

"Didn't do anything," Mama says.

Through the meal you watch her. She only eats a little. The look in her eyes is like before, strange and far away, frightened now and then. She is continually staring into the living room. When someone speaks, she listens, though nothing she hears changes any part of her expression. The more you watch her the more you feel dread yourself, and even when she tries to smile you feel afraid, though you don't know why.

Grove says, "I saw a piece of snow while we were running from Papa."

"He means he saw a flake of snow," Amy says.

"Amy saw it too," Grove says.

"No I didn't."

"You said you did."

"No I did not. You said you saw it, and you asked me if I saw it. But I never said I saw it."

"It fell right under your nose. Mama, is it going to snow?"

Mama looked out the window and slowly nodded. "The way it looks, it's bound to. It's cold enough on the ground."

"I hope it snows all day long and Papa gets stuck somewhere and can't get home for a week."

"Your Papa will get home one way or the other," Mama says quietly. "You ought not to wish bad things on him."

Duck says, "I hope he don't keep us awake all night again."

Mama rubs her forehead. "Nothing we can do about it, son. If he does, he does. If he don't keep you awake, he'll keep me awake."

"I hate him sometimes," Duck says, but Mama lays

her hand across his mouth. Grove says if it snows he's going to make a snowman with a rifle in the front yard, so Papa will see it and be too scared to come home. Mama says for him to hush too. "Don't talk about Papa for a while," she says.

A moment later Grove whispers, "Maybe you can make snow cream."

Finally Mama laughs, and for a moment her face clears. "I don't have any vanilla flavoring. You can't make snow cream without that."

"I bet Papa would get some at the store," Grove says.

"I bet he would too," Mama says.

IN THE living room you watch television with your brothers, listening to Mama and Amy clear the table in the next room. From the sound of Mama's voice you can tell when she is near the table and when she is beside the sink. You can almost guess the look on her face. "Rinse them good," Mama says, "and stack them in the sink. But don't drop any; I've been saving them dishes for the longest time."

"The pots need to be rinsed before this stuff dries on them," Amy says.

"Leave them to soak," Mama says. "I'll wash them and put them away when I feel like it." She sits in a kitchen chair, near the sink maybe, with the sweater wrapped close round her. You hear the clanging of pots in the sink, and Amy says, "I could wash them fine by myself if I could reach the durn hot water."

"Don't say 'durn,'" Mama says. "What would your teachers think about me if they heard you say a word like that."

"Oh Mama, I got better sense than to say 'durn' in front of my teacher."

"Better not to say it at all," Mama says, and stands in the doorway. Grove lies on the couch, head submerged in a vast pillow, a bag of ice resting against his elbow. He watches television quietly though anyone can see he doesn't like to lie still. Mama asks, "Is that ice melted, honey?" and bends to touch the bag gently.

"It feels okay," Grove says, though without looking at her.

"There's more ice if you need it changed."

"The cold makes it feel good," Grove says.

"We got to take care of you, don't we?" Mama says, stroking his forehead.

"He's spoiled," Duck says.

"I am not."

"You are too. Allen Ray lets you shoot the BB gun more than anybody."

"Don't talk about that stupid stuff now," Allen says. "Mama doesn't feel like hearing it."

"Watch TV," Mama says. She kisses Duck's white forehead. "Is there a good movie on, or is it just football?"

"This is a western," Duck says. "And then there's a monster movie next."

"I want to watch that, if it's scary," Amy says, coming to the door. "We ain't watching no stupid football."

Moving toward the window, Mama says quietly, "I wonder why they would show a monster movie on Thanksgiving Day."

"To give all the regular movie stars a day off," Duck says, and Grove laughs, and Allen says, "That's so stupid."

"I think I'm going to lie down," Mama says.

"You probably better rest while you can," you say.

She looks out the window again. You know she is staring at the road. For the moment the only sound is the wind. Grove lays back his head and closes his eyes. Mama checks the kitchen and kisses the top of Amy's head, for cleaning so well. Amy makes Mama hold her for a moment, and closes her eyes too. "If I could get to the shelf I'd put them away," Amy says.

Mama strokes her hair. "Leave them where they are and go sit down. You've done plenty."

Mama turns away again, watching the highway a long time. Allen asks her if she sees something but she says no. It rests her to look at the trees and the clouds, she says. Arms folded, she drifts to the bedroom, and Amy helps her put on her nightgown. Amy comes back a little later, closing the door.

You glimpse your mother through the doorway before it closes. She stretches out on the bed, pale as the sheets except for her dark hair. Unconscious of anyone watching, she lies like a child, curled in a tiny ball. Her face contracts as if with some nagging pain even when she closes her eyes. If you called her softly now she would hear you at once, even if you stood in the farthest corner of the kitchen and whispered. Mama never sleeps but that she listens for the least sound.

She lies frightened as something to be sacrificed. She brings her fist up to her mouth. Even after Amy closes the door you can hear her breathing.

White Time

In the afternoon darkness closes over the house, and the wind increases. High in the trees you hear a crying of many voices, a blended choir; almost, now and then, a sob.

A car passes on the highway once, and later, a truck drives by and makes everybody's breath catch, until you whisper from the window, "It's not Papa." Amy stands with her hand on the doorknob, ready to wake Mama at a moment's notice. All of you pretend to watch television, but you yourself listen beyond that box of noises.

Mama's breathing becomes deep and regular.

After a while you see some motion at the window and it makes you rise up in terror, you hurry to the glass expecting to see your Papa.

But snowflakes have begun to beat soft down along the world. Your whispered, "It's snowing," is hardly needed, your brothers and Amy see what you see and crowd beside you at the window. "Oh my God," says Amy Kay, "I can't believe my eyes."

"Now the roads will get icy," Duck whispers, but Amy shushes him. Everyone looks at everyone. Grove comes to the window too, propping his swollen elbow on the sill, holding the ice against the skin and watching the snow. The snow tumbles and spins, a wash of white, enormous motion across the fields, over the tops of the trees, blending sky and earth to complete whiteness like a fallen cloud. Duck presses his nose against the glass. His lips leave a print, from outside snowflakes brush against it. "I wonder if it will stick," Allen whispers.

"It's plenty cold out there," Grove says.

"It's cold enough in this old house for it to stick, if the snow could get inside," Duck says.

"We should listen to the weather report," Amy says, peering up at the eaves. "I hope it makes great big icicles."

"Like the ones in a cave," you say.

Grove leans his forehead against the glass. "It's all over the ground," he says softly. "You can see it everywhere."

"Boy, even if there was school tomorrow, we wouldn't have it," Amy says.

"Is it snow on the highway too?"

"I can't tell."

When you step back from the window they go on talking, and someone takes your place; no one notices you at the door. They chatter about schoolbuses sliding smack dab into ditches but you don't join in. You watch them a moment. Then you turn the front doorknob and go.

Outside the cold blast of air is a kind of fire, and hot

tongues of wind lick your skin. The snow is collecting on the porch, laces of white over the gray concrete. Wind whirls the flakes and tones hollow notes in the trees. Everywhere the clouds have thickened, the sun is a patch of paleness, not even a distinct disk. You have stood there watching it with the front door open, but now you open the screen and step out, hearing Amy say, "That crazy fool is going to turn out every bit of heat in the house."

By then Grove has followed you. The two of you stand arm in arm in the cold. Out here you can see snowflakes miles away in the pale light, tumbling down across the whole world. In the yard the flakes hover atop the dry grass. You dream them shattering against each other, soft silent breaking all around you, though when you taste one, cold and furry on your tongue, you are glad they are too soft to break, you understand snowflakes can rest easy on each other, their touch is light.

Grove says, "It's so cold out here I don't even need an ice pack on my arm."

"I never saw anything like this," you say.

"I wish I could fly around in it," Grove says.

"But even the birds don't fly around in snow," you answer.

At the door Amy says, "What if Papa comes home now? How can we lock the door with you two fools standing on the porch?"

"Papa won't drive nowhere in this mess," you say.

"He might. You never know with Papa."

Grove says, "We don't want to come inside. You can lock us out here if you want to."

She watches you, silent. You lift your hands to catch a snowflake that slowly melts in your palm, and then another, and then another, white dissolving to a tingle and a spot of water on your skin.

"The snow makes my arm feel good," Grove tells Amy.

"The snow makes everybody feel good," Amy answers.

"Except Mama doesn't like it much," you say.

"Well maybe she'll like this one." Amy steps onto the porch beside you, crossing her arms as the wind strikes her, making her squint and even drawing tears from her eyes. "It's so cold," she says, blinking, and Grove laughs, and you say, "What did you think it was going to be?" She sticks her tongue at you. Snowflakes strike her all over, washing her hands and arms, till at last she laughs.

Across the yard you watch the crystal gathering, the whiteness spreading, and the snow falls now so thick and fast it makes you dizzy, as if the world is moving upward toward the snow and the clouds.

Snow gleams in the forks of tree branches and along the roof of the house.

Soon beyond the river somewhere the sun is setting unnoticed behind the solid clouds. Millions of flakes of crystal drink the light. Out in the woods the snow is drifting down in even sweeps across and between the trees, collecting on the last leaves and on the ground. Beside the river the snow settles on the bank, along the bed of honeysuckle, a white lace beside the dark water. You wish you were there. Turning your face upward to let the cold flakes fall on it, you can almost imagine you are walking through a whole world of gray tree trunks and white snow, in twilight with the river beside you and the clouds piled so thick that even when darkness comes you cannot see the stars. You like the whiteness most of all. You would like to lie face down in the snow; you would like to gaze into the whiteness.

You shake your head at the cold, laughing, feeling the beats of your blood going off like a bomb, though you cannot even feel the hurt in your shoulder anymore.

"I wish we could play in it," Grove says.

Over his hair he wears a white veil.

"If you played outside in it you'd fall down and that would be the end of all of us," Amy says. But smiling, she finishes, "It don't hurt a thing to stand here and watch, though."

She leans far out over the porch edge, one arm encircling a post. She sticks her tongue straight into the air as far as it will reach, and closes her eyes and smiles. "Ash," she says. Grove laughs. You say, "You're the one who's going to fall and break your neck, Amy Kay."

She ignores you, sticking out her tongue and cooing. "This is what I like to eat," she says, "this is my favorite food. Nice cold snow falling straight down out of the sky."

"It doesn't fall straight," you say, "the wind blows it around for miles and miles."

"Mr. Know-it-all," she says.

The wind rises again, and cold soaks through every part of you. Amy says, "I'm so cold I can't hardly move." Grove shivers and hides behind you. The shivering hurts his arm. You see that on his face though he says nothing. "You ought to go inside," you tell him, and Amy says, "We all ought to go inside, before we catch pee-new-monia."

"I'm staying out here," you say.

"You don't have on enough warm clothes to stay out here," Amy says.

"It's not that cold."

She has some smart answer to throw back at you, but the wind freezes it in her throat, smashing her skirt into a tangle and ripping through her hair, tossing bales of snow against the three of you. Grove edges toward the house holding his elbow, though there is still delight in his eyes. Amy stands square on the porch stroking snowflakes out of her dark hair. Shivering, she says, "Well you can do whatever you want to, crazy person, but we're going inside and shut the door."

YOU WATCH the snow alone then, feeling easier in the silence. The snow drifts down from the clouds and piles against the earth, the gentleness of its drifting and piling giving you rest in some deep place. You take long breaths of the cold air, smelling the fresh, sharp smell of the evergreen at the side of the porch. You hunch your shoulders forward and blow out breaths that blossom into white clouds.

Finally descending the steps, slowly and carefully, hearing your Mama's voice in your mind.

But out in the full fall of it you don't think about being careful any more. The snow is all around you, falling slowly, close so that you can see the fluttering of particular flakes spinning over and jerking back, or far away so that you can watch the thousands descending, one great mass.

You trudge around the house, quiet under Mama's windows but wondering, still, if maybe she lies a little easier under the blankets, facing the window so she can watch the snow; maybe it eases her the same as you.

Above, clouds, and you imagine stars behind them, displeased to be kept from watching, maybe arguing with the clouds.

The grass beneath the snow crunches when you walk on it. The snow cools your shoes and then your feet. You blow into your hands.

Almost night. Almost dark. There, across the fields, over the gaunt line of pines, easing down against the house, vast fields full of the reflection of white, the snow settling to soothe the cracked earth, the broken cornstalks.

You wish you could lie in a bed of snow, let your head fall back into it slowly and never come out of it. You wish you had fire to warm your hands. You wish the snow would never stop, you wish Papa would never come home, or you wish you were in the middle of that field, out in the open space where the snow could swoop down at you from every side, seeming more and more endless; you can almost see yourself, turning and turning in the widening fall of the snow, lifting your arms and then bringing them down, as if you and the snow are one creature. You wish you could find a field wide enough that if you stood in the middle of it you would never see another house, where you could watch the snow pile higher and breathe the cold air deeper and deeper till your insides are as cold as your outsides.

You walk slowly across the open yard, you stare straight up into the falling flakes where you can see forever deeply into the one cloud. Almost dark now. Though you have seen the house and fields this close to night before, you have never seen anything like this, in motion, and you feel yourself rising with the same slow steadiness that the snow falls.

Above the snow, though, a sound. A droning, a motor, the approach—you half turn toward it—of a truck, headlights blaring, and you run into the front yard, almost to the ditch bank, to see.

Papa drives slowly past the house, honking his horn again and again, wipers beating away the snow.

If he sees you he makes no sign. He drives past the house, honking the horn always on the same beat. At Mama's windows the curtains stir, and a hand pauses at the glass. The red lights of the truck vanish down the road.

The curtains settle into place again. The day becomes quiet night. You walk away from the empty road to the house, wondering when he will come back to stay. Round you snow drifts like ash stirred up by wind, cold ash from a cold fire, a slickness that you carefully travel across.

Transpossession

In the kitchen you stamp snow from your shoes onto a torn paper bag. Amy fusses in whispers that you must be a fool to run around in the yard like you don't have the brains to know hot from cold. "Maybe you ain't as smart as everybody thinks," she tells you, gesturing with a spoon. "I think maybe you're a moron. I'm fixing you a cup of hot coffee to thaw out your belly."

"Papa drove by the house," you say softly. "Did you hear him?"

After a moment, Amy nods. She lights the burner on the stove, careful of the flame. "I guess he'll be coming home soon."

The house is mostly quiet. In the living room your brothers watch television with the sound turned low. The murmurs from the vague screen throw a hush over the room. Your brothers sit in a line on the couch. Once Grove asks if it's still snowing and Allen answers yes, he can see it falling through a crack in the curtains. Duck says he hopes it snows a whole six feet, though Allen tells him not to be stupid since it don't even snow that much at the top of a mountain. They keep their voices soft even when they disagree, and they watch the silent bedroom door. From Mama's room you do not even hear the whisper of breath.

Amy says quietly, "Pull off them wet shoes. This coffee water is almost hot."

"I don't want to drink any coffee."

She shakes the spoon beneath your nose. "Don't argue with me. You can put sugar in it."

"Even sugar don't make it good."

"It ain't supposed to be good. It's supposed to heat up your gizzard."

You step out of your shoes and sit at the table. She spoons the instant coffee into two cups and pours the water over it. Steam rises. "I'm going to drink me some too," she says, "sitting right at the kitchen table like I'm thirty-five years old. You can drink yours there too, and we can pretend like we're too old for TV."

"Let me put the sugar in mine. You don't ever put enough."

"You put in so much it might as well be syrup."

"Who's drinking it, me or you?"

"Don't leave your wet shoes right in the middle of the floor either. You won't raised in a barn."

You set the shoes in the corner and get canned milk from the refrigerator. Mama drinks her coffee black and Amy drinks it with sugar, so she can look like a grownup, but you like your coffee light brown. You watch the swirls of white in black, spinning and widening at the same time. Amy says, "Drink it before it gets cold."

"When I feel like drinking it, I'll drink it." You blow across the top. When Delia was here, she poured coffee from the cup into a saucer, and drank off the saucer like a cat. You sip your coffee from the cup like you're supposed to. The hot makes you swallow fast. Today you like the taste. You like the quiet too, with the refrigerator humming and the gas heater hissing, its firebricks bright red and glowing hot. The lights are dim in the living room, and Amy has left the kitchen dark. Snowflakes tumble against the windows. "I bet Papa is miles away," Amy says.

"I don't care how far away he is as long as he isn't here," you say. "Maybe he'll stay gone a long time."

"He might," Amy says mysteriously. The same impulse comes to both of you and you look at his empty chair. You don't have to be afraid of the living room now. You could even sit in that chair if you wanted to. The thought of the snow outside comforts you too, along with the silence it has brought to the highway. Though maybe you listen a little too hard. Too many things can sound like the motor of a truck. Amy laughs softly, raising her arms over her head. "We could pile up all the snow for miles around and build a big old wall to keep Papa out of the house. Except he'd just pee on it and melt a hole so he could get in."

When you laugh she signs you to be quiet. But you smile at each other. You hold the warm cup in your hands. Amy is half done with her coffee, though you have sipped only a little of yours. "I'm going to fix me another cup," she says. "Then I'll stay awake all night long."

"You will anyway, whether you drink coffee or not."

"Then it won't be different from last night, will it?"

"I wish I could go to sleep and not wake up, no matter how loud he yells. Except then I'd be scared to wake up and see what he did when I was asleep." You stir the coffee again, to make the sugar finish dissolving. Amy lights the burner on the stove and sets on more water to boil. She passes her hand through the steam. "You didn't leave me enough sugar for a mouse," she says, tilting the sugar dish for you to see that it's almost empty. You drag a chair to the cabinet to get down the bag of sugar. When you lift it your shoulder gives you a sharp pain. You set the sugar on the cabinet, the white grains sticking to the tips of your fingers. Amy holds the sugar bowl close to the bag, pours the sugar and then puts the bag back where it belongs. By the time you sit down your coffee has cooled and you can drink it faster. "Is it still snowing?" Amy asks your brothers in the living room. Duck stands at the window, gripping the curtain in a fist. He says, "It ain't falling as fast as it used to."

"If it don't keep falling there won't be enough of it left on the ground to keep us out of school Monday," she says.

"It's piled up over everything," Duck says.

"One good sunny day will melt it all."

"It's snowing for miles and miles," Duck says. He presses his face to the glass. "It's not ever going to stop, and Papa's never coming home."

When Amy takes her coffee to the living room you wonder if you should follow. You hold your own cup and swirl the last of the coffee around and around the bottom. You drink it and set your cup on the sink. In the darkness you gaze at the velvet window, where one tumbling snowflake appears and whirls against the black glass. You wish it would stay this way, so peaceful and quiet, with Mama asleep in the bedroom and none of your brothers or sisters arguing. But Duck says, "Here comes a truck," loud enough for you to hear, and you go to the living room and watch at the window with the others.

The truck lights blaze on the falling snow. You can barely see the shape of the truck behind. But you know when you hear the horn that this is Papa driving slowly past. From the bedroom you hear muffled footsteps. Mama opens the door, a gray shadow. "Come away from the window," she says softly, "you're standing too close."

You let the curtains fall and follow the others to the center of the room. The fire in the gas heater shines. Mama slips to the window buttoning her house robe. Her dark hair tumbles over her shoulder. She stands to the side of the window and watches. "He's not going to stop," she says.

"He came by here one time before," Allen says.

"I know. I wasn't asleep." Mama closes the curtains but still watches through the crack that remains. The truck's red tail lights round a curve and vanish. The highway shimmers with snow. Mama sits in Papa's chair, thumbnail between her teeth. She asks Amy Kay to bring her some Anacin. She rubs her forehead and takes a deep breath. The dark bruise glistens on her face. She takes the tablets from Amy's white hand and swallows them and sets the water glass beside the chair. Amy offers to make her a cup of coffee and Mama says yes, thank you. You watch her clotted figure in the light from the window.

From the couch you feel Grove's gaze, and you bring him fresh ice for his arm. He thanks you without moving. He asks, "Are the doors locked?"

Amy answers, "I pushed a chair against the door in the back bedroom."

Mama stands, holding the coffee listlessly. "I'll check the windows," she says. She pulls her sweater around her arms, letting the sleeves dangle free. She walks from window to window, watching the reflection of her face in the glass. You follow her from room to room. In her bedroom you press your face to the glass and smile at the lightened fields. The moon is a pure white shining in the clouds. "There's so many drafts in this house it's a wonder we don't all blow away," Mama says softly from the back bedroom. She stands in the middle of the floor shivering. "This room is so cold. How do you younguns stay warm enough?"

In her bedroom you study the tangled blankets on her bed. You hear her soft step and follow her through the door. She watches the highway, holding the coffee cup so close to her face that the steam envelopes her eyes. The snow has slowed. The flakes are smaller now, points of light that hang in the air. High in the clouds, the moon's patch is brighter than a moment ago. The clouds are breaking. On the highway you see tracks of tires.

"Did we check the screen door on the porch?" Mama asks.

"I locked it," Allen says.

"That little lock won't stop Papa," Duck says.

Mama sits in the chair again and sips coffee. You take her place at the window. When you lay your head against the glass the cold cuts like a nail through your brain. You study the snow in the roots of a sycamore. Someone turns the television louder. The blue light colors the room, soft on your brothers' still faces. Frail laughter bursts from the box, but your brothers don't laugh.

When you turn to the window it is as if you know he is coming.

Lights on the highway wavering in the snow.

"The truck is coming again," you say.

Amy turns off the television. When Mama lifts the curtains from the window you can smell the soap she used to wash her hands. Gently she pulls you back from the window. This time the truck goes slower than before. You become afraid when he approaches the driveway. But Mama merely watches, fingering the edges of the curtains. "He's driving past," she says calmly.

He honks the horn in front of the house, and you count the regular bray, once every four heartbeats, echoing in the silent room. The sound surrounds you and you shiver. Mama lets the curtain fall shut and paces the center of the room. Amy and Allen go to her and make her stop, embracing her as high as they can reach, but you are afraid to go near her. She gazes at the tops of their heads, her face drawn and pale. She watches the red lights through the curtains.

When Papa vanishes you watch the field of snow. The clouds have broken into rags and the snow has stopped falling altogether. Across the rain-eroded rows in the fields and the deep ditches dug in the dark clay banks lies the perfect whiteness. While you watch it part of you is dissolved in it, and you are not afraid, you are blank. But you know such absolute emptiness will never last.

In My Religion

There Are No Laws

Amy tells Mama she should go back to bed again, and get some more rest. "It's no telling how late he'll keep you awake tonight," Amy says. "Lay down and close your eyes."

From the chair Mama answers hoarsely she gets no more rest lying down than she does sitting up. "I hear noises in the dark," she says. "Half the time I think he's outside my window, listening." But she stands from the chair, goes to Grove and touches her palm to his forehead. At last she says, "Call me if you hear the truck."

She checks to see if the door is locked. You watch her disappear into the bedroom, the door closing without a sound. As soon as she is gone, Amy gestures for everyone to come close. "Don't sit there like fools," she says. "Papa could come back any minute. We got to keep watch."

You boys look at each other. Amy hisses for you to pay attention. She assigns each of you to a different window. Grove is to watch from the living room where he can still lie on the couch. Allen gets the side window in the dark pantry. Duck gets the window over the kitchen sink.

He can pull a chair up to it so he can see out, Amy says. She will take the window in the back bedroom. As for you, since you like to stay outside so much, you can keep a lookout from the back porch. You can see all the way to the river from there.

For a moment you watch each other, feeling like grown-ups. You troop off to your positions. Amy leads you on tiptoe through Mama's room. Light from the window outlines Mama's still figure. Her smooth arm covers her face.

Amy gets to the back bedroom ahead of you. She stands by the door to the porch with her hand on the knob, smiling softly. You put on your coat and she opens the door for you. She kisses you lightly on the forehead as you step out into the cold.

You turn and face the darkness. The first stab of the freezing wind makes the bone of your shoulder cry out. You huddle in the corner beside the wall of the house, sitting atop an old stove in the shadow. The stove has rusted orange and stains your pants, but at least the seat is dry. You count the eerie shadows in the back yard: the shed full of rusted tools and pieces of wagon wheel, the light perched on the tall pole beside the cedar, the old truck chassis, the clothesline, the trash barrel. Now and then a snowflake drifts through the air near the light. You count the flakes. You peer out as far into the dark as you can, to see if your Papa is standing somewhere out there. It would be like Papa to stand in the dark fields and watch the house where no one can see him. The yard is empty. You can't be still now that you have thought of that. You have to stand where you can see the whole sweep of the river.

Queenie prowls in the snow beside the bottom of the steps. When you open the door she stands, tail thumping, as if she knew you would be coming. You step down carefully and scratch her behind the ears. She sticks her wet nose in your hands. The yard is silent and overcomes you: you stroke the dog to warm your fingers. You lead her around the corner of the house where Duck can't see you both from his window. In the shadow you kneel to take her ears in your hand. You gaze across the fields.

At first you see only a gulf of blackness. The moonlight shines behind a thickness of clouds now, so that you are only gradually able to distinguish the field from the woods beyond. If he is there you only have to be still and wait. The cold encloses you, your breath hangs close. Moments pass. Once you almost turn to go back to the porch, figuring Amy could see him from her window, if he should appear. But then, against those distant trees, a momentary small fire flares, far off in the corner of the field. Someone has struck a match and thrown it into the snow.

Wherever he stands he blends into the trees. Even though you saw the light you cannot see him now, he is a shadow among shadows. But you know he is there somewhere and you freeze in your place, watching. You might see him if he moves. You back slowly to the wall of the house and kneel in the snow. It wets the knees of your jeans.

You wait for a long time. Once you glimpse a gray rhythm like legs walking, but it disappears. Up the road you think you might see moonlight on the windows of the parked truck, but still the fields are bare.

Then you see Queenie. Wagging her tail at the edge of the field, staring at a point in the darkness. She lopes across the white furrows, and after a while you see where she is running: toward Papa, far off in the snow, a tiny darkness.

High on the wind you hear him whistling.

His good arm arcs at his side as he walks, and he carries something that gleams.

Queenie brushes against his leg. He stops and looks down at her. The bright thing becomes still, a simple curve, and you do not know what it is until a glimpse of star-whiteness on a polished edge tells you the thing is a blade, is a knife, is cold and wind and moonlight joined in his hand.

He pets Queenie for a while. Lays the flat of the knife on her back. Says something that the wind garbles to nonsense. Has he seen you? You flatten yourself against the house. He is walking again now, and Queenie cocks her head when he leaves her.

You have to tell them you have seen him.

Papa can cover ground like a snake.

You slide along the house staying in the shadow. You hook the screen. Inside when you shut the door Amy turns to you from the window.

"Did you see him?"

"Look out there in the fields," you say softly. "Near where the back road is."

The light goes out of her eyes. She turns to the window. "Come show me where."

You press your face against the frozen glass. When you point you watch the slow tightening in her face. "He's got something in his hand," she says, and slips from the room like a shadow.

You find her beside Mama's bed. You stand by the windows peering through the curtains. When Amy whispers the news Mama rises from the bed in her nightgown. She puts on the housecoat and an old sweater. "Can you see him?" she asks you, standing above you. You answer, "He's by the clothesline now." Amy stands behind you both and stares at the floor. Her hands have tightened to white fists. Papa stands dark against the snow. He hides the knife behind him as if he knows he is being watched. As you raise your head to tell her what he carries, she says, "Go make sure all the doors are locked, Danny. And send Allen Ray and Duck to me, Amy. We're going to put some furniture in front of the doors."

Papa lifts the clothesline to walk beneath. The knife glistens with frost. Mama simply watches it and gives you both a push. "Do what I told you," she says.

You run to the back bedroom and bolt the door. Shadows move in the room. You feel a prickle on your neck. But only when you turn do you see the window, the curtains drawn, and Papa's glittering face watching you from beyond the glass.

You flatten against the door. You hear footsteps in the bathroom and call out, "Don't come in here."

In the doorway Allen stops short. You pretend not to see him. You stare at your Papa through the window, and he sees you and doesn't move. His harsh voice grates against the glass. He raps the pane with the handle of the knife and you look away. He sneers. A moment later Allen whispers, "He's gone."

Together you and Allen pull the chest of drawers against the door. The work makes your shoulder throb.

The chest of drawers had stood against an extra door that led directly to the kitchen. Mama had wanted to nail it shut. But now you unbolt it and beyond, in the kitchen, Amy nods her satisfaction.

"Papa was at the window in here," Allen whispers. "He saw Danny locking the door."

Outside, the sound muffled through the window and wall, something heavy lumbers against the porch screen.

"I hooked it," you say.

"He can break the hook," Amy answers.

"But we put the chest of drawers right up against the back door."

"This house has too many doors," she says

You hear the screen give way like Amy said it would, and then you hear heavy footsteps on the porch. Papa curses when he bangs against the old stove where the snake plants and ice plants sit. But he cuts the noise short. Steps quietly. You can hear him breathing. Suddenly in the dark the paint and shadow form a good man's face hanging in the air. Papa scratches the door softly. You picture the edge of the knife and Papa whispers something, and you touch the image of the man's face and murmur words of your own, and just as the knife squeaks on the metal doorknob Allen whispers, "Don't let him in."

A moment passes, another, and another. Papa lumbers down the porch and back into the yard. You take Allen's hand and drag him into the living room. There you see Amy on her hands and knees. She glares up at you. "Don't stand there, help me. Mama don't remember where she left her shoes."

From the window Mama says, "He's at the side of the house. He's got that dog with him."

"Queenie?" Grove sits up straight.

"I'll beat her half to death for being with Papa," Duck says.

You run to the window yourself and gaze at the snow-covered yard where your Papa stands dark with the dog at his side wagging her whole body with delight. Now you can see Papa's cool smile.

Mama's face washes white with moonlight.

You hear the thump of Papa's footsteps on the porch and then hear the rattle of the doorknob. He never makes a sound, till suddenly the door crashes with thunder. You see it jerk and bow in, the chair set against it bucking away. Mama steps to the doorway and watches.

You think kitchen to bedroom to bedroom to living room to kitchen.

Perfect circle of doors.

You children all watch her and no one really sees when the door finally gives way. Cold wind whirls in. Papa lurches past the chair. His voice is low, almost a growl. You can see how drunk he is by the way he weaves as he stands. "Lock me out of my own goddamn house, will you?" He does not have to raise the knife, everyone watches it. When he lunges toward Mama she vanishes into the kitchen, and he is right behind her, the whole house trembling with his steps.

The circle is a wheel, you are under the center, the hub is an eye looking down as you look up.

You hold the curtain dumbly and hear your mother start to cry.

When she rushes through the living room again her terrified gaze rakes all of you, and you see the slash in the arm of the sweater, though no blood on the gown inside. Papa follows after her, but smiles and turns to catch her in the other direction. Amy shouts, "He's turned around, Mama," in a clear falling voice. Amy ducks into the kitchen under the table when Papa turns to her. You can hardly breathe when he looks at you. But framed in the bedroom door you see your mother's shadow, wrestling with the chest of drawers.

She can't get out of the house because of the chest. Now he is chasing her again, and she runs, and you run behind them both through the bedrooms, holding your breath. In the back bedroom you silently struggle with the chest of drawers till you have it far enough away from the door to get it open. Your shoulder throbs. Steps sound behind you, and frightened cries. You unbolt the door and turn the cold knob at the same moment that you hear your mother in the other bedroom, and when you open the door he has shoved her against the bathroom wall and laughs because he thinks he has caught her. But she sees the open doorway and the light from outside and runs toward it.

Papa blinks as if he doesn't know what happened. Then, before you can think to move, Amy is there, grabbing your arm and you and the rest gather blankets from the bed, pull on shoes and coats, spilling out into the moonlight and the snow.

The cold bursts against your face. Ahead of you Grove runs across the snow, with Duck at his side to catch him if he falls. Grove frowns at every step and cradles his elbow tenderly. Amy and Allen wait under the last of the sycamores, blankets across their shoulders and hair tangled by the wind that sweeps in from the fields. Amy wraps a blanket around Duck and Grove, and Allen hands one to you that you clutch against your shoulders. The wind almost tugs it out of your hands.

From the porch you hear the sound of cursing and footsteps.

"Hide behind the tree trunks," Allen whispers.

"Where is Mama?" Duck asks.

The wind rushes through the fanned branches overhead, a crying in the dark nets of shadow, the moon broken through the clouds and riding a clear black sky.

Papa hawks and spits.

Has Mama gone under the house again? No. A thrill runs through you. Only turn your head. There in the snow-planed field Mama runs through the stubble corn toward the swaying shadows of the pines.

You hear Papa start to run and then you see him, and something cold rises up in your throat.

The silver flashing up and down.

You step away from the tree and so do your brothers, but Amy is the first into the field. You run and run and then, far off, Mama sees you and stops still. She waves you back, but cannot wait to see if you will do as she says. In the deep snow her steps falter. Papa's longer legs carry him faster; he is a flattened shadow along the ground. He closes the gap between them and you think he will catch her if she can't go faster. Amy calls out for her, and then so do you all, and Papa stumbles in the snow. Cursing, he rises, glittering white, and runs again, but Mama vanishes into the dark forest, her white gown dissolving into shadow.

Ahead, Papa kicks free of another cornstalk and crashes to the ground.

Amy calls you all to her side. "We better not get no closer," she says. "Mama can't hide with five younguns to look after."

"Is he going to kill Mama?" Grove asks, but no one answers.

Papa roams the snow back and forth in front of the place where Mama disappeared. His steps wear a dark path in the snow. Over the wind his deep shouts carry clearly. "I'll find you, you goddamn bitch. I'll find you if I have to look behind every tree that ever grew!"

Allen moves closer to Amy.

"I know you hear me," Papa shouts. "You better run if you want to get away." He stretches out his good arm and the silver shines. "But don't think your children will get away. I got them right out here in the field with me. You see them, don't you? You ain't going nowhere as long as they're here, don't you think I know it? You always would have traded ten of me for one of them."

A stirring in the bushes, a flash of white. You feel your heart rise.

Papa sees the movement and rushes toward it.

But when you see the wagging tail you know it isn't Mama, it's Queenie. She breaks free of the bushes and trots toward him.

When Papa sees her he stiffens.

He speaks more softly but you still hear. "You are a bitch just like this dog," he says. Queenie sniffs his ankle, watching him talk. He lays his knife against her head. "You are exactly like this dog, do you hear me?" His arm rises with that gleaming at the end. From far away the motion is only a tiny arc of silver, but to Queenie it must seem like thunder when that silver blade descends. Again, again, again. Only after a moment do you understand what he has done. By then you can feel it all through you.

He lifts the limp dog by the hind legs and throws her flopping end over end into the forest.

Afterwards he stands as if he is listening. He stares at

his hand a long time. He kneels to cover the dark place in the snow with whiteness, stands still holding the knife, turns it in his fingers, no longer gleaming.

You don't even know enough to be afraid.

Mama steps out of the woods and calls clear, "Are you finished now, Bobjay?"

He turns sluggishly. The knife dangles.

Mama walks neatly through the snow. He shouts, "I ought to kill you," but Mama pays no mind to him, walks wide of him and comes to you. With relief she kneels and embraces you, turning your faces up to hers. "Walk real quiet and calm," she says. "He doesn't know what he did."

"Are we going to stay here?" you ask softly.

She simply looks at you. "Where would we go? Just walk, that's all we can do. Real quiet and calm. Don't look back at him."

The Lay of Wrath

She closes the door when you have come inside, and switches on the faded lamp between your beds. She makes Grove lie quiet on the cot at the end of one bed and stands watching him. "Does your arm hurt much?"

"No ma'am, it's still so cold."

"Amy, wrap him up some snow in a towel."

Amy marches off silently, fetches a towel, and opens the back door tossing her hair. When she comes back she says, "Papa's standing right where he was before."

"I expect he's surprised with himself," Mama says, not looking at any of you.

Amy settles the towel gently against Grove's bent arm. "He's wicked," she whispers. "He's like the devil."

Mama shakes her head. "You ought not to think your Papa is a bad man."

"He killed Queenie," Duck says. No one answers. You close your eyes to stop from seeing it again, but it does not stop: the dead thing spins as it flies into the trees. Mama says to get ready for bed. In the middle of putting on your pajamas you hear the front door open and close.

Heavy footsteps resound through the rooms. When Mama looks at you her eyes have that look of dullness again, and you ache to send that look away. Papa is in the other bedroom by now. Staring at the unmade bed. Now you hear him in the bathroom. You turn your face away from that doorway. You watch his shoes. His voice rakes along your skin. "I wondered where all of you were," he says.

Mama says, "It's time to put the younguns to bed."

He says, "I reckon so."

"Go sit down and I'll make you some coffee when I finish." She buttons Grove's pajama top and settles the cool towel into place.

"Is our baby sick?" Papa asks.

Mama swallows when he comes too close. But her voice never falters. "His arm is swelling. But I'm keeping cold on it."

Papa nods his head and lumbers away. You step to the door and watch his back darken and disappear. Mama gazes at Grove and strokes his forehead. She pulls the covers over all of you and kisses each of you on the forehead. Almost as if she were kissing you good-bye. When she turns out the light you hear her footsteps recede endlessly far. You gaze at the ceiling and feel the dark night swell.

For a long time you lie awake listening. The house is quiet. Everyone's breathing makes a different sound, you could count them separately. Once or twice you hear the heavy thud of Papa's footsteps and wonder where he is walking. You hear the quiet click of Mama's careful tread, but never at the same time as Papa's. You picture her watching him from corners, near doors. She waits for him to sit down before she goes into the kitchen. You picture the match she strikes to light the stove, igniting with a small hiss. You gaze into the darkness overhead. Something turns over and over deep inside you. Except for Mama making coffee you hear nothing but the wind at your window. A brush of snowflakes from the sycamores. You picture Mama beside the window drinking her coffee. You know she is standing because once Papa asks her to sit down, and she whispers she doesn't want to, she can't keep still, she's too nervous. He goes back to his chair. She is silent. You picture her gazing through the window at the snow and the moon, maybe at the arcs of light on the crusted tree branches, steam from the coffee rising into her face. Maybe she wishes she had curled up in a blanket out there in the woods. Maybe she would not mind going to sleep in the cold either. She sips her coffee and takes deep breaths. A long time passes. The house makes few of its usual noises. Beside you Allen, exhausted, has fallen asleep. You hear Duck's regular breathing, and Grove's as well. Amy makes no sound. You hear Papa's deep cough, you hear the chair creaking, the flare of a match. Later Papa asks Mama to help him pull off his shoes and after a moment she does. You hear them drop to the floor. Silence falls again. Mama steps nervously from kitchen to living room. You picture her face passing out of light into

shadow. The house falls so calm you can hear the refrigerator humming and your own heart counts moments into
the night. Though the room is pitch dark you can see
everything in it clearly. Grades of shadow from the beds,
the coats thrown on the floor, Duck sprawled in the blankets, Amy sleeping with her mouth open. Grove turning
restlessly, murmuring. Allen curled up in a ball touching
no one. The quiet does not ease you. In the living room
you hear Papa shift in his chair. Mama comes to the bathroom, scrubs her hands in the sink.

Suddenly they are talking. Their voices are calm. Measured bits of conversation, and silence between. Now and
then you hear a word you know: your own name sometimes, or Grove's, or Queenie's, or Delia's later: the sound
passing through your head like a stream. Vague images
flicker in your mind: Delia laughing in the kitchen, the
orange dress limp on the clothes hanger, Mama's white
hands on the front door, the silence when she closes it, the
moonlit field, Queenie's body spinning over bushes. You
remember the softness of the earth under the house, the
sight of Papa's legs, the pieces of glass and the cold biting
your skin. You hear Papa walking again, and Mama saying, "I don't feel like coming to bed right this minute." The
words flow distantly overhead. After a while Papa's weight
sinks slowly into the mattress in the next room. Your own
heaviness mixes with the silence that follows. It might have
been that you fell asleep. Though even there you keep watch
on the darkness with your sleeping mind, and nothing
moves in any room that does not raise some image in you.

Mama walks restlessly in the living room wondering about the morning. Papa turns on the groaning springs and coughs. Coughs so sharp the sound almost wakes you: a hand that retreats in the darkness from touching your shoulder. Someone watches you sleep tonight, you turn over and over. You can feel somebody staring in the dark from far away. Maybe you know Mama waits in the living room hoping Papa will fall asleep before she has to go to bed herself. Though to tell the truth she must have waited many nights that way, before and after this night, and maybe some of your memories are only dreams of other nights; maybe when you are sleeping you can feel all nights, past and present, stretching ahead and back for many years.

You toss and turn, and this time when you touch Allen it is you who are repelled.

Papa's cough punctuates the night, lifting you close to wakefulness again. A match strikes. In some dream you are having, you picture the flash of orange. In the living room Mama stiffens and closes her eyes. In the silence she can feel Papa waiting. Still she sits by the window, watching the clear light fall onto the snow like white fire. Everywhere the emptiness summons signs: a flash of headlights on the road, the drift of a pale cloud overhead or in the silent house the creak of a spring, the heavy fall of a footstep. When Mama hears it she has been expecting him for some time. Papa comes to the doorway and asks, "When are you coming to bed, honey? It gets so cold in here by myself."

"I'm not tired yet," Mama says, keeping her back to him.

"It's no wonder you don't sleep, as much of that coffee as you drink."

"I need it to relax," Mama says.

"But I need you to relax," he says.

"If I came to bed I couldn't keep still. I'd turn over and over all night."

After a pause Papa's voice changes. "Turn around and look at me."

"Please leave me alone, Bobjay. If you lay still for a while you'll fall asleep."

"I can't rest without you. You know what I mean."

Mama hugs herself to keep from shivering. "I don't think I could stand for you to touch me right now."

"I didn't ask you whether you could," he says quietly.

She says good-bye to the white snow on the yard and beyond. She lets the curtains fall into place. When she turns she has already begun to count her breaths.

He has the knife. He holds it so lightly. He himself leans against the doorsill, smiling so earnestly. His pale, hard flesh shining. He reaches to switch off the lamp. In the darkness he speaks so softly his voice reminds Mama of a cat purring. "Come to bed with me. It's late."

He gestures with the stained blade. She takes a deep breath and shakes her dark hair. The thought that she might run again makes her smile. She walks calmly past him into the other room.

She watches the window. When she hears his footsteps follow after her, she tells herself she can get through this, she will live. When he lies on the bed behind her, she feels the mattress sink down. Now gravity pulls her toward him too, and she swallows. The moonlight spills softly thorugh the window, washing silver over a patch of floor. Now the whole house is dark and quiet. From the back of the house she can hear you children breathing in your sleep.

"Lay down," Papa says.

The wonder is, when she turns, the knife does not make her afraid. She might long for it, if it would bring any rest. She says, "Put the knife down," and he blinks at her. He lays it on the sheets. When he settles back against his pillow she can't see it. He is smiling, though; it will be all right. He leans toward her, the good hand descends gently to touch her and she holds her breath. But she shivers when she feels the hand on her. Oh please, she thinks, help me to be still.

But in the end nothing can stop her from trembling and drawing away. He draws away too, and watches her darkly. She whispers, "I don't know what else you expect, after today."

"You're my wife," he answers. His voice resounds. She starts to tell him to be quiet so he won't wake up the younguns, but he covers her mouth with the good hand. He slides against her. She tries again to let her body go, to let him take it. But past his shoulder she sees knife again. It makes her think of the white dog. For a moment she is in the woods, parting the leaves with her fingers, watching as he bends over the dog and lunges and lunges and at last flings the dead thing spinning. Its shadow crosses the snow. She hears the fall behind her, she does not know how close until she turns. Queenie has come to rest in the root of an oak, and Mama bends over the body counting the deep wounds, the torn belly heavy with burst life. Now this same man kisses her neck. The smell of him thickens and rises all through her. He asks, "Why do you act so cold?"

She answers, "I am cold."

"Let me make you warm," he says.

But the smell is too much, she backs away, and something darkens in his eyes. "Who are you dreaming of now?" he asks. "Who is it you want so much tonight that you don't want me? I saw the bed won't made when I came back."

She answers, "There isn't anybody to dream of."

She draws a sharp breath when he touches her gown. "There's got to be something keeping you so cold to your husband."

She says, "You don't have any idea what that could be?"

"I have some ideas."

She looks him in the eye and says, "I don't want to be close to you. I can't stand it. I would rather you killed me like you killed that dog."

"I didn't hurt that dog," he says. His voice swells and rings. In your sleep you stir, Danny, as if you know. She feels his stillness before it frightens her. He rises and she sees what he is reaching for. In his face the same coldness and sharpness as the blade. "I never hurt that dog," he says. "I never hurt you either." She is transfixed by the thing and the look on his face, and for no reason she thinks of him when she first knew him, when they were first married, and she sees without doubt that his face was softer then, that he has changed to become this, that he has changed for good. He raises the piece of arm, the blued end. She half-rises from the bed, but suddenly he is leaning over her and she cannot move. The knife shines close to her chin. Something in his eyes makes her think he doesn't know her any more.

When he raises the knife her body floods with a wash of coldness. Her blank cry rising, a perfect silence, that this simple blade and act and night might become everything, that there might be nothing after this. Her furious heartbeat reminds her *breathe, breathe*, and she watches him hovering close. The sob she sobs catches all of her, and she hears him laughing. But it is not him. She has never been so far away before. She knows the knife is cutting through her gown. The tip of the blade is cold.

He smiles but she is not sure she is looking at him. She is looking at nothing, she is looking at the ceiling and the receding shadow. His voice follows her. "I'm not good enough for you," he says, "I'm scum, I'm some kind of bitch you don't want to touch," he says, "ain't nothing good enough for you except your children," he says, "you love them three times as much as you love me." She makes a low cry as the keenness slides along her skin. "You ain't had a minute for me since the day they was born."

She says, "I'll fuck you, please stop."

He says, "Oh no, I'm not good enough for you, I'm not your real blood kin."

She says, "I'll do whatever you want, please."

He says, "But you only like it with your kin. Well I can get some of that for you right now."

You must have heard, Danny, even though they kept their voices soft; you must have heard, because this call is for you.

You will remember the footsteps, or maybe the sound rises out of memory even as you hear the coughing in the bathroom.

Though maybe the memory really begins when he touches your sore shoulder. Suddenly you are awake and you rub your eyes. Maybe you make some soft sound. When you recognize him, leaning down over you, you stiffen. He shakes his head thoughtfully. "Come on," he says in a voice that rumbles through your bones. "Your Mama wants to see you."

There is something you want to ask him, now, while there is still time.

But he lifts you like some lifeless doll and you do not make a sound even though pain flashes through your shoulder. He carries you pale through the cold room where Mama waits with the sheets tangled around her, watching you and watching the knife in Papa's hand. It is not much of a journey. It only leads you where you would be anyway if your Mama had slid past your Daddy in time.

No Distance,

Only Clouds

In the morning when you wake, white light is filling every corner of the bedroom, outlining each bleached plank of the walls, coloring Amy's arm folded in the blanket. When you sit up, careful of your shoulder, you can see the side yard from the window. A clean layer of whiteness covers the familiar ground from the house to the fields beyond, more perfect and unbroken than you would have imagined. You feel full of something like peace. For a moment you cannot remember why it seems strange to have wakened in your own bed.

Then you do remember, and whiteness closes over your mind.

You are riding in the dark with your face against Papa's stubbled neck, you can smell the sweat in his T-shirt.

Allen stirs beside you, mumbling you ought to lay down before the cold air runs under the blankets.

You listen for any sound from the rest of the house.

Then you hear voices in the kitchen, Mama and Papa talking quietly as if this were any morning, as if yesterday had never happened, and you wonder how your Mama can go on talking to him like that.

Allen says, "Lay down Danny, I'm cold," and so you do, but it is hard to breathe because you are afraid. With snow on the ground Papa might not have to go to work.

You hear Mama say once, "The water won't get hot a bit faster than I can get it hot," and Papa laughs.

When you close your eyes the pattern of the yard and snow-covered field is reflected in what you see against your veined eyelids. Since you cannot distinguish words in what they are saying any more, the sound of their words becomes like a river washing you, and the thought of that is like another kind of whiteness. You are tired, you drift into something like sleep.

You dream you are lying in the crook of a tree.

Far below, the golden lion lashes his tail and watches you.

You had been playing with him in the clearing, he would like to go on playing.

Your thigh is bleeding from deep gashes that run the length of the muscle, and you are dumbly watching the blood ooze out from the marbled flesh. You have only stray thoughts, like whether you would be more comfortable if you could break off some branches to cushion your head, or why the lion's eyes are such a golden color. Meanwhile the big cat shakes his mane and sniffs. He thinks your blood smells delicious, he wants some. He wants to play with your body a while in the grass and then taste your tender thigh. He is watching you with that eager impassivity, that simple hunger. From the base of the tree he calls out to you, a throaty rumbling, and he shakes his mane and parades from side to side.

But at the moment when River Man would have entered the dream to save you, the sound of your Papa's voice and footsteps penetrate to you and you sit upright in the bed.

Papa has come to the bedroom door. He stands with his back to the doorjamb, watching you with a fixed intensity. You swallow and take deep breaths. You are surprised to learn you are not afraid of him, you are able simply to contemplate his sober aspect, his neatly combed hair and freshly shaven face. He watches you and you do not flinch. Finally he asks, "What do you think you're looking at?"

You answer, "I don't know," and your shoulder throbs where he gripped it, fingerprints of pain.

He frowns and turns away. He says, "Go back to sleep like you're supposed to," and you do lie down in case he stops to peep at you from beyond the door.

The sounds of his voice and footsteps cause Duck and Amy to stir restlessly in their sleep and Grove wakes at the sound, sitting up, watching you.

Papa's heavy footsteps round the circular house.

Grove whispers, "I wish he would stay away from us," and you nod, but now you can hear Papa's voice again and it is hard for you to breathe. He is saying something about Queenie. The dog's name is the only word you understand, but when you hear it a sudden restlessness consumes you.

You get out of bed quickly so the cold air will not disturb Allen, asleep again with his mouth open and one arm shading his eyes. The glass dresser-drawer knobs are cold to the touch. The folded clothes inside have your Mama's smell. You are careful not to disturb the ordered piles but you dress as quickly as you ever have, considering you can hardly move your shoulder at all. Your coat is hanging ready in the closet. When you pull it over your sweater Grove says, "You ain't supposed to go outside this early. It's snow on the ground."

"I don't care." You button the plastic buttons with some difficulty, the pain in your shoulder makes your fingers move slowly.

Grove says, "I'll tell Mama."

"No you won't."

"Yes I will."

"You ain't going anywhere near Mama while Papa's in there, you can't fool me."

Grove considers this and lies down in bed again. "I'll tell her when she comes to check on me."

You stand over his bed. His swollen elbow rests on a thick feather pillow and his eyes are dark from troubled sleep. You say, "Lie down and be still. I ain't going anywhere but to the river."

"What do you go to that old river so much for?"

"I ain't ever seen it in the snow."

The back door is beyond his bed. Cold pours through the window glass, through your corduroy sleeves; cold from the doorknob pierces the bones of your arm.

Grove says, "I was awake last night. I heard what Papa did."

Winter light is pouring around his shoulders, throwing shadows across his face. You say, "I don't want to talk about that," and you remember, for an instant, your mother's face, the tangled sheets, and you shut the image away, opening the door.

Grove waves good-bye solemnly as if you are taking a long journey.

On the porch you move as if Mama is already hunting for you. The back of her head is visible above the tin of black pepper resting in the windowsill. You crouch low beside the table that holds the ice plants. Through the walls Mama's voice travels to you clearly, though she is speaking to Papa. "I reckon if you can drive around blind drunk in a snowstorm half the day yesterday you can drag yourself to work this morning." When she moves away from the window, gesturing to Papa with a bottle of syrup, you slide through the screen door and round the corner of the house like a wraith.

Here you can pause and rest. Out beyond is the white world you watched from your window, only full and broad, smelling of pine from beyond the fields and another smell, acrid smoke rising from a pillar in the trash can. Mama has already burned the trash this morning.

Beside the cinderblock underpinnings are your footprints from last night. Here is the place where you peed in the snow. You walk beyond that to the side yard and the fields.

Now you can see the tracks from last night, where Papa chased Mama across the field and where you children followed, but in the morning light there are not as many footprints as you would have thought. The wind gathers at your back. You can almost picture the moonlight on Papa's shoulders as he stood shouting into the forest.

You shiver and walk in another direction, toward the river road to the clearing where your brothers were shooting birds yesterday. You walk with your head held high as if you are a grand prince with your ermine-lined cloak thrown over your shoulders, your expression serene as if you are dreaming. Only once, when you happen to look down, you note that you are crossing a trail of crisp dog footprints, a single sere line headed toward a particular point in the middle of the field.

You walk more quickly toward the river, but you cannot escape the image that follows: first the dog spinning in the air and then your Mama again, twisted in the sheets, watching you as Papa holds you above her, and watching the knife in the same hand that holds you, Mama frightened but saying, "Be careful not to cut him, Bobjay," and Papa making an odd sound, like a sigh, when he strips down the sheets and sets you on her belly. Mama not seeing you at all then, Mama watching the knife and then closing her eyes, turning away and pressing her hands flat against you to keep you from touching her breasts.

You take a deep breath and shake your head clear.

The ground is icy. You calculate each step, certain you will not fall. No one needs to tell you to be careful. No one needs to tell you anything. When Mama's image tries to reappear you shake your head again. It passes. Only the icy ground remains, and nothing there can harm you.

Inside the pine forest there are heights where you would like to soar, rooms you can see far above, formed of icy branches, curved arms of crystal that would embrace you; but you are far too heavy to float in the air.

Soon you reach the river. The moss is crystalline, treacherous to the foot, so you get down on your hands and knees and crawl till your knuckles are blue. You reach the train trestle, the bed of honeysuckle vine, and you sit there with your legs crossed like an Indian, hands folded in your lap. The trestle is silent. You picture a dark train plunging toward you down the icy tracks, guided by a fierce light, driving your crushed body deep into the earth; or you imagine River Man rising out of the black water, ice dripping from his muscular chest and arms; he kneels, finds you wounded in the honeysuckle and carries you down to the bottom of the river. You are certain he is in the black water somewhere, as certain as if you could see him.

Maybe you will walk down to the bottom of the river to find him. But for now you are content with the cold and you wrap the brown coat tight, stretching the sleeves of your sweater over your fists. Still the cold rises from your blue jeans into your thighs, your marrow. You sing quietly, *Shall we gather at the river, the beautiful, beautiful river?* and you know, and you do not know, which gathering the song means.

You sit there a long time. At one point, from far off you hear the sound of a truck driving away from the house, down the long road. You know that means your Papa is going to work and so you smile. But it is only a little noise from here, and even now you are content to sit still on the snow-covered vine. You do exactly that long into morning, frozen in a trance, singing the same words over and over while now and then a branch falls from far overhead, a cracking like glass or like the cry of a bird struck by a copper BB pellet.

A long time passes. The river blackens. The gray sky threatens more snow. You contemplate the numbness in your legs. The snow is as white as the sheet that tangled your mother's arms.

Suddenly a voice calls, "Danny," and your ears tingle.

When you turn you will see the lion, golden mane tumbling down like flame.

The voice calls you again and you turn serenely, smiling.

Only it is not the lion. It is your Mama walking through the snow in the red dress, trudging through the snow in Papa's old work boots with her white sweater clutched tight against her. The red dress glows. A bruise is purpling over one of her eyes. When you see that you find your voice. You call out, "I'm over here, Mama," in a hoarse voice and she hears you and turns.

She simply watches you. Her arms relax a little. After

a while she says, "What are you doing out here in the cold, son?"

"Looking at the river."

She walks toward you slowly. "You been out here a long time?"

"Yes ma'am."

"Are you cold?"

"Yes ma'am."

She is standing closer now, beside a sapling that long ago curved over and grew into the ground. Her features soften. You know what she is remembering. She asks, "If I told you to come here, would you do it?"

You say softly, "Yes ma'am," again, and slowly unbend your legs. They are numb from the cold and will not hold you up. Mama watches you struggle and hesitantly comes toward you over the bed of vine. Gently she massages your legs till blood and warmth return. "You been sitting on the cold ground too long," she says, but there is no admonition in her voice, she is tentative instead, and handles you as if you are more fragile than ever. "How is your shoulder?"

"It hurts," you answer, "but not that bad."

"Do you want to go home?"

"Is Papa coming back?"

"No. Not till late I don't expect."

So you walk with her. There is no sense of hurry in either of you, and you shyly take her hand and lead her through the places that are familiar to you, that are your treasures in this house, so she will understand why you come to the river. You do not sing now, but soon she is humming a hymn you do not know, and she tells you it is from the Holiness Church she went to when she was a little girl.

When you are near the edge of the woods, though, you both hear a sound and it stops you cold. A truck is approaching from far down the highway. The sound of the truck is as familiar to you as your own breathing.

You and Mama step behind the bushes that fringe the woods. Papa's truck does appear, but it passes the driveway to the house, passes the yard and field. By the edge of the woods the truck stops and the motor becomes silent. Papa steps out with the empty sleeve to his coat tucked into his pocket.

He watches the field for a moment. Then he pulls a shovel from the back of his truck, hefts it across his shoulder and jumps over the ditch. He walks slowly down the edge of the field, peering into the woods, and finally he pauses before a stand of bare dogwood, branches shaggy and white.

Mama motions for you to follow her and you do, without a sound, keeping behind the cover of the undergrowth.

It is easy enough to find him, in a clearing where two green fir trees stand in a circle of dogwood and cedar, all evenly laden with white. Papa is digging a hole. The ground is hard and he has trouble managing the shovel, but his face is grim and you know he will not be stopped by mere cold earth. You can hear that he is saying words.

Mama nods and watches, kneeling with the sweater stretched around her to hide the dress. You watch too, and after a while you understand what he is doing.

Beyond him is Queenie, lifeless, twisted curiously as if she had been leaping to catch one of your brothers' fallen birds but fell back to earth herself, frozen in arc. From the distance you cannot even see her wounds.

When the grave is deep enough, Papa lifts Queenie tenderly, nearly stumbling on the slick snow but cradling the dog even then, lowering her stiff body into the grave, and Papa goes on mumbling words.

Mama's eyes are closed, and her mouth moves silently. Papa covers Queenie with the pile of cold dark earth. Afterwards he stands for a while, studying the house across the field. Never once does he look toward where you and Mama are hiding.

Papa says audibly, "You better forgive me for this. You said you would." He could be talking to the trees, or the clouds, or the empty air.

After a long time he returns to his truck and drives away. The sound dwindles, vanishes to nothing, and still Mama kneels in the snow without moving.

Finally she walks to the freshly turned ground where Queenie and her children lie. Mama stands there for a long time. She touches the heaped earth with the toe of one work boot. At last she says, "I don't reckon he could help it," and looks at you.

You realize this is all she will ever say. You remember again the motion of her eyes closing, her head turning away, denying, when Papa brought you naked to her bed; and suddenly you understand. In that moment against her dreamy lids floated the image of her own River Man, and while Papa held you against her she dreamed of a world in which you and Papa and all the others had never existed. You know this in your bones, not in words. So when she asks you, almost shyly, "Are you ready to go home?" you are able to say yes at once. You are able to follow her willingly across the snow-covered cornstalks, to say yes ma'am when she tells you to be careful. You are able to take one breath following another. What your eyes tell you is news. Mama is a frail woman in a red dress walking across a field toward a house where the doors open into a circle, room on room on room. You are a little boy following your Mama across the field. She has found you by the river and brought you home. You did not go down to the black water where River Man was waiting. But you will return to the river for as long as you live in this house, and now when you choose your path you will pass the clearing where your Papa has buried a dog. The grave will be like a channel marker, and when you are there you will know that facts are your only friends.